The Trouble with Weddings

The Trouble with Weddings

BEVERLY ♥ LEWIS

Zondervan Publishing House
Grand Rapids, Michigan

A Division of HarperCollinsPublishers

The Trouble with Weddings
Copyright © 1993 by Beverly Lewis

Requests for information should be addressed to:
Zondervan Publishing House
Grand Rapids, Michigan 49530

Library of Congress Cataloging-in-Publication Data

Lewis, Beverly, 1949–
    The trouble with weddings / Beverly Lewis.
      p. cm. — (Holly's heart series ; bk. 4)
    Summary: Thirteen-year-old Holly's life is complicated by her
mother's upcoming second marriage, her best friend's crush on
her cousin, and boy troubles of her own.
    ISBN 0-310-38081-2 (pbk.)
    [1. Remarriage—Fiction. 2. Cousins—Fiction. 3. Christian life
—Fiction.] I. Title. II. Series. III. Series: Lewis, Beverly,
1949– Holly's heart series ; bk. 4.
PZ7.L58464Tr 1993
[Fic]—dc20   93-7943
                                              CIP
                                              AC

Edited by Lori J. Walburg
Cover design by Cheryl Van Andel and Johnson Design Group
Cover illustration by Tim Langenderfer

Printed in the United States of America

93 94 95 96 97 /   / 10 9 8 7 6 5 4 3 2 1

To Aleta Hirschberg,
my sweet Auntie 'Leta,
whose mother-heart
has touched hundreds
of Kansas schoolchildren
. . . and me

♥ Author's Note ♥

Thanks to Julie, Niki, Janie, Becky, Allison, and Amy for reading the manuscript, and for giving me tons of cool suggestions!

Thumbs up for my Monday night SCBWI group including Mary Erickson, Vicki Fox, Carol Reinsma, Peggy Marshall, and Barbara Reinhard, who offered valuable assistance on the manuscript, as well as Barbara Birch and my husband, Dave.

Cheers to Lori Walburg, for her enthusiasm, encouragement, and expert editing.

O N E

A bad case of curiosity made me tiptoe down the hall to Mom's bedroom. I held my breath as I listened for the slightest sound of her early morning activity. No way would she allow snooping. Not in a zillion years!

My fingers touched the cool doorknob as I glanced over my shoulder, ears straining. All clear! Slo-w-ly the door glided open, and I crept into her rose-colored room, neat as always. Scanning the room, I spotted it—Mom's latest greeting card from Uncle Jack. It stood on the antique pine dresser beside the lamp. I reached for it, a twinge of guilt tickling my conscience.

Pink rosebuds danced around the edges of the romantic card. Dying of curiosity, I turned to the inside. Just as I thought. The note at the bottom confirmed my suspicions. I read the words. *I'm counting the hours till I see you again, Susan. Love, Jack.* A red ink heart twinkled up at me. Uncle Jack was no artist, but the happy face in the middle said it all: Jack Patterson was in love with my mother!

Creak! The steps! My heart pounded as I put the card down on the doily near the ceramic lamp. I crept to the door and peeked through the crack. Mom had reached the top step and was making the turn into the hallway leading to her room.

Yikes!

I stepped backwards, away from the door, darting here and there searching for a hiding place. Where to hide? In a flash I scampered into Mom's walk-in closet. I spied her huge clothes hamper. *She'll never find me there!* Slithering inside, I yanked the dirty clothes out from under me and covered myself with them as I waited, listening.

"Holly! Time to get up for school," Mom called at my door, halfway down the hall. Lucky for me I'd left my bedroom door shut. She wouldn't call me again, even if I didn't answer, at least not for a while.

Her pumps squeaked as she approached her room. Inside, she hummed, swooshing the curtains aside. *She's in some fabulous mood, today*, I thought, secretly congratulating myself for finding the perfect hiding place.

One of Mom's pet peeves was nosy people. She wouldn't be singing now if she'd discovered me snooping! I could almost see her—wearing one of her many wool skirts with a sweater or vest to match, her shoulder-length blonde hair swept up or back, away from her face. She was probably settling down for her devotions about now. I could almost hear the pages of her Bible turning as she found the verses for the day.

Mom loved her quiet times. It felt good to know she spent time with God before going to work at the law firm where she was a paralegal. It hadn't always been that way, though. But now all of us were Christians. All but Daddy . . . and his new wife.

Good thing there were tiny slats in the side of the hamper, or I'd be suffocating by now. My legs were scrunched. How much longer? Sooner or later Mom would be wondering why I wasn't up and in the shower.

Br-r-ing! I jumped as Mom answered the phone. Lifting the lid, I eavesdropped. Mom would freak out for sure if she knew I was in here.

"Good morning, Jack," Mom cooed.

In spite of the pain of being hampered in like this, I grinned. Things were perfect. Mom was dating my favorite living relative. His wife, my aunt Marla, had been Daddy's sister. *She* used to be my all-time favorite relative, but she died of cancer last February, three days before my thirteenth birthday. It was a nightmare for all of us . . . as bad as when Daddy divorced Mom.

Last month, Uncle Jack surprised us when he moved his consulting business from Pennsylvania to Dressel Hills, our ski resort town in the middle of the Colorado Rockies. Best of all, Stan, Phil,

Mark, and little Stephie—our cousins—were only a few blocks away. And Mom was happier than ever—well, at least as happy as when Daddy lived here.

"Tonight?" I heard Mom saying. "I'll have to ask Holly first, but I'm sure she won't mind."

Mind what? I closed the hamper lid silently. My knees were frozen now, my neck stiff. If I didn't get out of here soon, I'd be late for school. I could almost see the principal shaking his head in disgust. No way would he buy a trapped-in-the-hamper story.

"Holly!" Now my little sister Carrie was calling me. "Wake up!" she yelled, pounding on my bedroom door.

I gasped. *This has to be the dumbest thing I've ever done!*

"Mommy, Holly's still asleep," she said, coming so close I could hear her shrieking Mom's name inches away from me.

"Just a minute, Carrie," Mom said. "I'm on the phone."

"But I can't find Goofey anywhere," she whined, like a typical eight-year-old. "He's *nowhere!*"

"I'm sure he's around somewhere," Mom said.

Carrie stomped down the hall calling, "Here kitty, kitty."

Scr-i-tch, scr-a-tch! Something was clawing the outside of the hamper. "Meow!" It was Goofey. He must have followed me in here. My heart sank.

I'm doomed! I crouched down and covered myself with laundry.

I heard Mom place the phone in its cradle. "Carrie, dear," she said as she headed toward the walk-in closet . . . and me. "I think Goofey's in here—in my closet." She opened the door.

I held my breath. *I'll never snoop again, Lord. I promise. Just please get me out of this mess!*

Scr-a-a-tch! Goofey pawed harder at the hamper.

"There's nothing to eat in there," Mom said to our cat. Her knees cracked as she bent down to pick him up. "Here, I'll show you," she said, lifting the hamper lid.

My heart stopped beating!

TWO

"That's strange," Mom said. "I'm sure I did my laundry yesterday."

A tiny stream of air escaped my lips as I exhaled inside the hamper, preparing for the wrath of Mom.

She continued. "See Goofey? It's nothing but a pile of dirty clothes." Goofey meowed again. Then . . . bam! Mom let the lid drop. "C'mon, let's get you some breakfast." Her footsteps grew muffled as they reached the carpeted steps leading downstairs.

"Close call," I whispered as I pulled myself out of the hamper like a butterfly struggling from its cocoon. Free at last, I flung the dirty clothes out of my way, limping out of Mom's closet and past her dresser. I blew a kiss at Uncle Jack's card. "It's all

14

your fault," I whispered, grinning as I headed for my room.

I found my journal in the bottom drawer of my dresser. I scribbled, *Wednesday, September 22nd: I knew it! Uncle Jack's in love with Mom. More later.*

I glanced at my watch. It was late. If I skipped shaving my legs, I could shower and be ready for breakfast in ten minutes. But . . . yikes! Tryouts for girl's volleyball was after school today. I *had* to shave. Danny Myers would be there cheering for me. How could I impress my new boyfriend and Miss Tucker, the new coach, with cactus legs?

In the shower, an idea struck. I would shave during lunch, in the girls' locker room. Perfect! After drying off, I tossed a disposable razor onto the back of the toilet. I grinned at the mirror as I brushed my teeth. If this morning's narrow escape was an indication of my luck today, I couldn't wait for tryouts!

At breakfast, Mom asked if I would baby-sit for Carrie, Stephie, Mark, and Phil that evening. "Uncle Jack and I are going out."

"Why can't Stan at least stay home with the boys?" I asked, gobbling down some cold cereal.

"Uncle Jack didn't offer to have Stan sit with Phil and Mark." She wiped the counter. "Stan must have other plans."

"Okay this time." I gulped down my orange juice. "Isn't this your second date *alone* with my uncle this week?" I teased.

Carrie piped up. "Uncle Jack used to let us all come along. Not anymore." She giggled.

I waved a napkin at my sister. "That was then, this is now!"

"Right," Mom said, wringing out the dishcloth. There was a twinkle in her eyes and a spring in her . . .

"Mom! You have a run in your hose," I said, pointing.

She stared at it in horror, then dashed upstairs to change. "We're running late, girls," she called down. "I'll drive you to school."

I swallowed the last of my orange juice and raced to my room to grab my books.

"Girls!" Mom called from her room. "Who's been in my clothes hamper?"

I froze.

"Not me," Carrie said.

"It's a mess in here!" Mom insisted. "Holly?"

I stretched my aching legs, remembering my hiding place. A high price to pay for snooping, especially on the day of volleyball tryouts. "It's really late, Mom. We *have* to go," I said ignoring her question and heading downstairs.

"I'm coming," Mom said. "Can't figure out what happened to all the dirty clothes in my hamper." She pressed the garage door opener. "It's the strangest thing," she muttered.

Settling into the back seat, I breathed a thank you heavenward. No more snooping for me! I intended to keep my promise.

I slipped into science unnoticed, grabbing the

nearest desk in the back of the room. My stomach rumbled as I glanced at the clock. Could I last till lunch?

I spotted Andie. She was wearing her jean outfit with matching jacket and purse. Did she have her usual package of peanut butter crackers stashed nearby? I sure could use a nibble about now!

I coughed, hoping to get my best friend's attention. She didn't turn around. I wrote a note, folded it, and passed it to the boy in front of me. He tapped Andie's shoulder. How obvious can you get? Andie turned around at the exact moment the teacher did.

Mr. Ross stepped to the front of his desk, adjusting his glasses. "Miss Martinez, please step forward."

Andie blushed deeply. Before getting up, she stuffed the note into her sock!

"What is the rule in my class concerning note passing?" Mr. Ross asked, sliding his glasses up again. I could see smudges on them as he stepped closer.

Andie cleared her throat. "It's not allowed, sir."

"And did you receive a note?"

"Yes, Mr. Ross."

"You broke the rule then?"

She nodded.

Mr. Ross looked past Andie at me. "Who else is involved?"

I couldn't let Andie take the blame. Standing up, I confessed, "I am, sir."

"Both of you will see me during your lunch

break," he said, then turned and went to the board to write down today's assignment.

Lunch? How would I have time to shave my legs *and* show up for Mr. Ross's lecture? A person could starve to death by then.

After class, my new boyfriend—Danny Myers— was waiting by the door. Almost fifteen, he was taller than most the boys in ninth grade. Logical and *very* spiritual, Danny possessed a unique quality that calmed me down. It was one of the coolest things about him. That and his amazing memory. His only flaw: Danny was a bit controlling sometimes—and preachy. I found that out last summer when we had an argument about my going to visit Daddy in California.

"Hi, Holly." Danny reached for my books. "Walk you to your locker?"

I smiled. "I need to *hide* in my locker." Then I told him about passing the note to Andie in science, but he assured me that Mr. Ross wouldn't make me miss lunch.

"I hope not 'cause I'm starved!"

He reached into his pocket. "Here, try these."

"Almonds?" I tore the tiny package open.

"They're quick energy, and good for you, too."

"Thanks." I smiled up at my health-nut friend. "Once again, you saved my life."

"My pleasure," he said, running his free hand through his auburn hair. "I'll walk you to your next class."

"Perfect," I said, spotting Kayla Miller posing beside her locker with that flirtatious grin. It made me mad—not her grin so much as her crush on Danny. The word was out; Danny and I were together, but that wasn't stopping *her!*

The almonds helped me make it till lunch break. By eleven forty-five, I was more worried about shaving my legs than anything else. Mr. Ross was sure to lecture away our entire lunch hour!

Andie waited outside the door to the science room. "Ready for this?" she asked.

"Sorry I got you stuck in the middle," I said.

"Don't worry. If we're polite, he'll let us off."

"You sure?"

"Just watch." She opened the door and sauntered in.

Mr. Ross sat at his desk. He slid those smudged glasses up his nose as we came in. "Please be seated." He gestured to the front row of desks.

Andie sat quietly, folding her hands on the desk. I copied her.

"Very well, girls. Let's chat."

He's going to drag this out forever, I thought as I tried to match Andie by faking an interested expression.

"Are the rules of this classroom clear?"

Andie nodded. So did I.

"Do you understand that there must be consequences paid for misdeeds?"

"Yes, sir," said Andie. Ditto for me.

"Very well. You will both write a five-hundred word essay on the importance of following rules. In short, responsibility."

No problem, I thought almost gleefully. A writing

19

assignment—the least possible punishment of all time.

I stole a glance at Andie. Poor thing. For her this was worse than grounding. She despised essays or anything closely resembling them.

"Mr. Ross, may I say something?" Andie asked.

"You may."

"The note I received from Holly Meredith wasn't willfully breaking the rule."

Mr. Ross raised his bushy eyebrows. "Oh? How is that?"

"The note was important. About matters of life and death."

"Life and death, indeed." He stood up, stuffing his hands into his pockets and frowning. "Please explain."

"Well, sir, Holly didn't get enough to eat this morning at breakfast. She just wanted to borrow a few morsels."

"Morsels?"

Was he falling for her story? I looked at my watch. *C'mon, Andie, hurry it up.*

"Are you saying your friend, here, is under-nourished?"

"Well, she *is* quite thin, as you can see," she said, pouring it on thicker than ever.

Mr. Ross looked concerned . . . at me! "We do have a social worker in the building three days a week. If you aren't getting enough nourishment at home, Holly, there are some avenues that can be considered."

Oh great, Andie, I thought. *Get me reported to Social Services, why don't you?*

I said, "Thank you, but that's not—"

Andie stood, interrupting me. "Excuse me. I really must get my friend to the cafeteria now."

I wanted to strangle her!

"By all means," Mr. Ross said. "And girls . . . the assignment tomorrow . . ."

He's going to cancel it, I thought.

". . . is due bright and early," he said with an air of finality.

Out in the hall, Andie groaned, "An essay! Look what you've done, Holly."

"*I* did? *You* made it sound like my mom neglects me."

"Sorry about that," she said as we rushed to lunch.

"You oughta be," I said, dashing through the line in the cafeteria, grabbing a sandwich.

"What's your hurry?" Andie asked, catching up with me.

"Have to shave my legs," I whispered, finding a table and making room for Andie.

Andie rolled her eyes. "Please, I'm eating."

I giggled. "Hurry, you can cover for me in the girls' locker room."

"For what?"

"For snoopers, while I take my jeans off and shave my legs in the sink."

"How bad are they?" She leaned over and slid my sock down.

"Get outta here." I playfully pushed her away.

"Why should I cover for you when you got me in trouble with Mr. Ross?" she said, reaching for her chili dog.

"Best friends do things like that for each other," I said. "Among other things."

"What's that supposed to mean?"

"Kayla Miller," I said. "Watch her for me."

"You mean spy on her to see if she's after Danny?"

"You got it," I said, clearing off my tray. "Coming?"

"I'll catch up with you in a second."

Racing to the girls' locker room, I glanced at my watch. Seven minutes to shave Sherwood Forest before Miss Wannamaker's composition class. I searched my purse for the disposable Bic razor.

It was nowhere to be found!

THREE

I made a mad dash around the locker room, jiggling one locker after another, searching for an open one . . . with a razor.

"Are you crazy?" Andie appeared by my side, hands on her hips.

"Frantic," I cried. "I forgot my Bic."

"Is *that* all?" She went to her locker, swirled her combination lock, and produced the precious blade. "Here."

"Thanks." I hugged her, then raced to the sink. "You're the world's best friend!"

"Now that I saved your skin . . ."

"And that's no lie!" I said, slipping off my jeans.

"Don't you think you owe *me* something?" she said.

I swooshed warm water and soap over my bare

leg. "Is this a hint?" I laughed. "'Cause if it is, I already know what you're up to, Andie."

"That's good, because there's no way on earth I'm gonna write that essay for Mr. Ross."

By the look on her face, I knew she was serious. "It wouldn't be honest if I wrote it." I skimmed the blade over my leg.

"Come on, Holly, this is not for a grade. It's a punishment!"

I grabbed a towel out of my locker. "Still, it'll have your name on it, right?"

"None other than. Look, I'm going to be late for class," she said, a little huffy. "See you at try-outs."

"Thanks again, Andie," I said, waving the shaver as she disappeared through the door.

♥   ♥   ♥

After school I hurried to the gym. A line of girls were already ahead of me. Most of them had played volleyball *last* year in seventh grade. Danny had warned me that the competition would be stiff, but now it hit me hard. My throat turned as dry as cotton, so I sped to the drinking fountain.

Kayla Miller was getting a drink. Her twin sister, Paula, stood in the line waiting for tryouts. "I think I'm going to throw up," Kayla said, holding her stomach and looking pale.

"What's wrong?" I asked, convinced she *could* be sick by the expression on her face.

"Just nervous, I guess," she said. "I have to make this team."

"You made the team back east, didn't you?" Paula and Kayla's family had just moved here last spring.

She nodded, her ponytail bobbing up and down.

"Then you shouldn't have anything to worry about."

She smiled faintly. "Hope so."

"Well, I've gotta run." I sprinted to the locker room, where I pulled on green shorts and a white top. Last year these shorts had haunted me with their ridiculously wide legs. Now, as I viewed them in the mirror, they almost fit. At last my scrawny legs were developing. At long last!

The new coach, Miss Tucker, stood in the middle of the gym floor, blowing her whistle. I ran my hand over my right leg. Smooth! Andie had saved the day. She showed up just then with Danny and Billy Hill. Billy was as cool as a guy gets. He'd helped me play a trick on Andie at my birthday party last February. Now he was her latest heartthrob and one of Danny's best friends. I waved them over to my side of the gym.

Danny lit up when he saw me. "Hi. How do things look?" He leaned against the wall beside me.

"Like you said, big competition."

"But *you're* ready, Holly." He flashed a smile at me. He was right. I was ready and had been for weeks. All those practice sessions last summer with Danny had paid off.

Kayla Miller was called first. I watched her

serve—like a pro. I swallowed hard, nervous, as she did her thing on the court. And *she* felt like throwing up?

Danny must've sensed my insecurities because he reached for my hand. "You're a natural at this," he whispered. "Remember *that*, Holly-Heart."

His hand felt good—made me feel more relaxed as he laced his fingers between mine.

Jared Wilkins wandered over. Something about the bounce in his step—and his crazy, fun-loving ways—still attracted me even though I was with Danny now. I wished my heart would stop beating so wildly every time my former first love showed up!

"Hey, Holly! Good luck out there." Jared's blue eyes twinkled another message. I wasn't sure what.

"Thanks," I said, looking up at Danny's face, wondering if he'd noticed Jared's subtle flirting.

"Excuse me a second," Danny said, heading for the rest room.

Instantly, Jared took Danny's place beside me. "You're a hard one to track down these days," he said.

I wasn't exactly sure what that meant. But then Jared wasn't the easiest guy in the world to figure out. One of the things I liked about him! I pushed a stray strand of hair back into my braid. "I've been right here in the gym ever since school got out today."

"I don't see you around much anymore." He leaned a little closer to me.

"Well . . ." I blushed. "Danny's been helping me get ready for the tryouts, if that's what you mean."

He arched his eyebrows. "Spending lots of time with Danny?"

"Ever since September 6th at 7:15 P.M.," I announced, remembering when I'd said yes to Danny in a letter.

"Really? That long?"

Danny was back, and he reached for my hand. "Wait'll you see Holly do her stuff out on the court," he bragged to Jared.

Jared nodded, taking note of my hand in Danny's. Then he winked when Danny looked the other way. I blushed again. A girl doesn't easily forget her first love, even if he *did* turn out to be a rotten two-timer.

The whistle blew, its shrill sound echoing off the walls. "Holly Meredith!" called the coach.

I sucked air in too fast and almost choked.

"Remember Philippians 4:13, Holly. You can do everything through *him* who gives you strength," Danny reminded me.

I smiled and headed toward middle court.

Andie shot me her famous thumbs-up. "Go for it, girl!"

No matter what, I promised myself I'd keep my cool. And I did! Setting up, spiking, bumping the ball—I was wired for this moment. Next I showed off my serve. After three good ones in a row, Miss Tucker asked me to put a spin on the next serve. I did it!

Thank goodness Danny had insisted I drill this. I could hear his voice above the crowd. "Yes! Go for it, Holly!"

Coach Tucker pulled me over after the rotation and patted me on the back. "Meredith, you're *good*." She lowered her voice. "Be ready to show up for practice tomorrow . . . three o'clock sharp." I wanted to hug her, but thanked her instead. It sounded like I'd made the team!

Miss Tucker blew her whistle. "Stan!" she shouted across the gym. "Cover for me just a second."

A tall blond boy emerged from the crowd. It was my cousin. "Good show, cuz," Stan said, shuffling the pages on his clipboard. "A little rough around the edges, but not bad."

I leaned over and pulled up my socks. "What are *you* doing here?"

"Didn't you hear? I'm the student manager for the girls' B team."

"Oh great," I muttered as I walked off the court, away from him. "Just great."

Andie screamed at me from the sidelines. "Holly, you were amazing!" Danny, standing beside her, beamed.

"Coach hinted that I made the team!" I called. Excited, my friends gathered around. Andie did a little jig before she hugged me, and Billy gave me a high five. Jared congratulated me next, but his smile faded a bit when Danny moved in beside me. Was he jealous?

After everyone left, Danny went to get his jacket

on the bleachers. "I'll call you tonight," he said, heading for the door.

"Okay. Thanks again for your help."

Danny nodded, turning around. Then he stared at me. Well, not really stared, just looked terribly pleased.

My heart skipped a beat as he waved good-bye.

FOUR

"Wow, Holly," Andie said, swinging her purse as we walked to the locker room. "You were hot today!"

"Thanks," I whispered to my toes.

"Hey, what's wrong?" she said, pulling on my sleeve.

"My *cousin*. He's the student manager for girls' volleyball."

Andie stopped cold in her tracks. She put her hands on her chubby hips. "Stan Patterson's your *cousin*?"

"Uh-huh."

"Why didn't you tell me? He's a knock-dead babe!"

"He's my cousin, silly."

"So? You have to introduce me."

"I do not," I said, opening my gym locker.

"Ho-l-ly," she whined. "I've seen him around school but didn't know this new guy was related to you."

"Well, he is." I pushed my bangs back.

Andie continued. "You promised you'd introduce me to him, before your Uncle Jack ever moved here. Remember last summer?"

"Faintly."

"Hurry and get dressed before he leaves," she begged.

"Have to shower first."

"Shower at home."

"No," I said stubbornly.

Then I saw that familiar glint in her eyes. She twisted a curl around her finger. Look out . . . trouble! "Have *I* got an idea for you," she began. "An even trade. You introduce me to your gorgeous cousin and I'll forget about the 500-word essay for Mr. Ross."

"You'd do that? Write your *own* essay just to meet my schizoid cousin?"

"You heard it here," she said, laughing.

The essay punishment was, after all, my fault. "Okay." I gave in. "It's a deal. But I've got the best end of it." I ran off to the showers. They were busy, but I managed to find a private stall. Soon I was back, dressing and brushing my hair.

Andie gathered up my dirty clothes and rolled them into the wet towel. She stuffed them into my gym bag. "Would you hurry?"

"Relax, will ya?" I fastened a clip in my damp

hair and headed out the door with Andie leading the way.

Back in the gym, Stan and Miss Tucker stood on the sidelines, comparing notes.

I sized up the situation. "Doesn't look like a good time for personal introductions."

"We'll wait," she said, locking her stance like a stubborn mule.

Almost on cue, Stan glanced up, motioning to me.

I nodded to Andie. "Now's your chance."

"Gotcha." She giggled.

We walked across the gym, our tennies squeaking. I introduced Andie to Stan. "I don't think you've met my best friend, Andrea Martinez."

"Hi, Andrea," he said. "Are you in eighth with Holly?"

She nodded, speechless.

"Andie, this is Stan, my cousin."

She snapped to it. "I've seen you with Billy Hill and Jared Wilkins. We all go to the same youth group at church. Maybe you could come with Holly sometime."

Stan smiled. I could tell he was studying her, but only casually. No way would he be interested in *my* best friend. Besides, Mom had said there was a girl back east he was writing to. "Maybe, sometime," he said.

Just then, Andie's mother showed up pushing a double stroller. She paused in the doorway with Andie's two-year-old twin brothers.

Stan turned. Before we could say a word, he had darted across the gym to see the toddlers.

"What's he doing?" Andie asked, surprised.

"Stan's a sucker for little kids."

"Really?"

"Not babies, little kids," I said as Stan knelt down to talk to Chris and Jon.

"Hi, Mom," Andie said as we followed Stan over. "Whatcha doin' here?"

"It was so nice out," she said. "Thought we'd soak up some of the September sunshine."

Chris bounced up and down. "An-dee-dee," he said, pointing his chubby little finger at his sister.

"He's desperate to get out," Mrs. Martinez said. Andie unbuckled him, took his hand, and walked him around the gym.

Stan unbuckled Jon and lifted him up, up— pushing his brown curly head high into the basketball net. Jon giggled and squealed for more.

"Here you go," he said, showing Jon a basket-ball, saying the word over and over, letting him try to hold it. Andie couldn't take her eyes off Stan, and neither could little Jon.

"It's getting late," Andie's mother said. "We'd better start home."

Andie helped put the twins' sweaters on before we headed for the door.

"Nice meeting you, Stan," Andie said.

"Same here," he said, waving at the *boys*.

Outside the autumn air was turning brisk. It was like that in the mountains. Summer was over almost before it got started in Dressel Hills, Colorado.

"I think I'm in love," Andie said on our way down the hill toward the city bus stop. Her mother pushed the stroller ahead of us.

"Have you forgotten Billy? He's crazy about *you*."

"Whatever," she said. "Call me after supper. I've got an essay to write." The bus pulled up to the corner, half a block away. She ran to catch up with her mother and little brothers.

The bus was filling up fast. "Better hurry," I called, strolling past the Soda Straw, sort of a fifties diner with a soda fountain and every flavor of ice cream in the world. Today it was hopping with kids, most of them from volleyball tryouts.

Kayla Miller dashed out the door, her ponytail bobbing up and down. "Holly! Wait up!"

I waited on the sidewalk for her to catch up. Her grin was gone. In its place were accusing eyes. "I saw what happened at the gym right before you and Andie left."

Puzzled, I made a face. "*What* happened?"

"Stan, uh, your cousin. You were talking to him."

Now I was really confused. "Maybe you better spell it out, Kayla."

"You introduced him to Andie, didn't you?" Her eyes squinted part way shut, like my mom does when she's upset.

"Yeah, so?"

She looked away. "You don't know this, but I've

34

been in love with Stan Patterson for as long as I can remember. Before we moved here, he and I went to different schools, but I always saw him at church."

I listened, still wondering what she wanted from me.

She continued. "Then Mrs. Patterson died and Stan's dad went to another church. I don't know why. Anyway, I never got to see him much after that. Now here we are in the same junior high, and he doesn't even know I exist."

I scratched my head. "Why are you telling *me?*"

"You're his cousin, Holly. You could set me up with him, right?"

First Andie, now Kayla. "I really don't know what you see in him. Besides, my best friend is bugging me to—"

"Your helping *her*, aren't you?" she interrupted. I nodded.

"That's all. Please, just set me up with him."

"But he *knows* you already, doesn't he?" I said, totally confused.

"Barely," she said. "Please, Holly?"

I burst into a stress-attack. "This is crazy! Stan moves to town and everyone's mushy over him."

"Because he's so-o cute," she crooned.

"Cuter than Danny?" Oops, I caught myself. Too late.

"Danny Myers?" she said. "He's okay, I guess but . . ."

"Then you don't like Danny?" I couldn't believe I said that!

"What makes you think that?" she asked, twirling her ponytail around her fingers.

"Remember last summer, Kayla? You practically begged Danny to help you with your serves. You flirted all over the place, even at the library."

"But don't you see? It was all for Stan. I knew he'd be involved with the girls' volleyball team this year. That's why I wanted to make the team so bad. Danny's just a friend."

"Really? Just a friend?" I didn't buy it for one second!

"So, will you?" she asked.

"Will I set you up with my cousin, is that what you want?"

She nodded, tears glistening in her eyes.

This girl's either completely lost it over Stan or she's the best actress around! I opened my mouth to speak—

"Holly!" shouted Andie, running across the street toward us.

"Andie?" I said, surprised.

"The bus was too full for all of us, so I let Mom and the twins go ahead. I'll catch the next one." She glanced at Kayla Miller. "Am I interrupting something?"

"Not really," Kayla said, wiping her eyes. Then looking me square in the face she said, "Call me with your answer tonight," and dashed into the Soda Straw.

"What was *that* all about?" Andie's dark eyes demanded an answer.

"Love, love, love," was all I could say. I turned

to go. How could I tell my best friend that the girl I suspected of chasing my boyfriend was really in love with my cousin Stan—Andie's latest heart-throb?

"Holly!" she called after me. "Talk to me."

"Later." I turned around, forcing a smile. "*Much later,*" I said under my breath as I trudged toward home.

F I V E

I kicked every little stone along the sidewalk as I headed home. There wasn't any big rush to get back. At the beginning of the school year, Mom had said since Carrie was turning nine next month I could take my time getting home. Besides, I was in eighth grade now, which meant more freedom.

So I took my time fuming over my stupid cousin, Stan. I was freaked out at the sudden interest the whole female population of Dressel Hills Junior High showed in Stan. Andie, Kayla . . . and who knows who else? I didn't dare tell him. He already had a mammoth ego without *this*.

Downhill Court—my street—came into view as I turned away from the ski shops downtown. Dressel Hills was a blaze of gold, the only fall color we had here in the Rocky Mountains. Back in

Pennsylvania, trees turned every imaginable hue. Here, people drove for miles to see the shimmering yellow of the quaking aspen trees nestled against the backdrop of dark evergreens.

When I got home, Mom was in the kitchen putting a casserole into the oven. "How were tryouts, Holly?"

"You'll never guess in a zillion years," I said, leaning my books against the sink and trying not to grin.

Mom tossed the hot pads aside and hugged me. "You made the team!"

"I still can't believe it."

"*I* can. After all the hours of practicing over at Danny's. How is he anyway?"

"He's really cool, Mom. He treats me fine."

Mom's eyes squinted half shut. "What's that supposed to mean?"

"You know. He's the coolest boy I've ever gone out with."

She looked like she was gonna drop her teeth. "You're going out?"

"Not really, Mom. Didn't I explain all that? Danny knows I can't date till I'm fifteen. That's just what we call it when we don't want to hang out with anyone else."

Mom set the oven timer. "Just so we understand each other."

"When's Uncle Jack picking you up?" I asked, moving my books to the long bar in the middle of the kitchen.

"Six o'clock. That's why I made chicken casserole. You'll be feeding the whole crew, minus Stan. Think you can handle things?"

"No problem. Except I do have lots of homework tonight." I was thinking of the essay on responsibility I had to hand over to Mr. Ross first thing tomorrow.

"I'm sure Uncle Jack will make it worth your while. He pays by the kid per hour, right?"

"Yep," I said, hoping Uncle Jack would keep dating Mom. It was good for business! And by her smiles . . . good for her.

"By the way, Holly, I'm planning a surprise party for Carrie—a week from this Saturday." Mom followed me upstairs to my room. Goofey our cat padded up behind me.

"Who's coming to the party?" I plopped down on my lavender canopy bed and snuggled with Goofey.

Mom closed the door, then sat on my window seat. "I'm inviting Stephanie, Mark, and Phil, of course, and Carrie's new friend, Brittany Lloyd from school."

"What about Zachary Tate? I know Carrie would love to see him again." I stroked Goofey's neck, and his purring rose to a rumble. I wanted to hear what Mom would say about her former boyfriend's kid coming over here.

She breathed deeply, slowly exhaling. "I don't think it would be wise. Zachary had a rough time when his dad and I quit dating. I wouldn't tamper with his feelings now for anything in the world."

I leaned back on the bed. "I never see Mr. Tate or Zachary at church anymore."

"I think they must've gone to another church," Mom said. "I really do miss having Zachary in my Sunday school class."

I bet she did! Mom had a strong mother-heart. If she and Daddy had stayed married there'd probably be a batch of us by now.

"What do you think about Carrie's surprise party?" Mom asked. "Counting Carrie there'll be five kids."

"Sounds perfect for a nine-year-old." I pulled out my assignment notebook. "I won't be able to help you with the party much. There's an ice cream social at the Soda Straw with Pastor Rob and the youth group. Okay?"

"Uncle Jack will be here to help me," she said. Suspicious-looking twinkles gleamed from her eyes as she mentioned his name.

I grinned. "You really like my uncle, I see."

"Is it obvious?" Mom said, fooling with her hair.

"Does Uncle Jack know you're in love with him?" *The question I'd been dying to ask.*

A smile danced across her cheeks. "Who wants to know?"

"Mom! Tell me!" I jumped off the bed and raced to the door, blocking her exit with my body. "You're stuck here till you tell me."

Mom giggled like a schoolgirl. "I better let you get to homework before the troops arrive." She touched my hair. "I really appreciate you, Holly.

You're so responsible. I know I can always count on you."

"No fair changing the subject." I moved aside to let her pass. She closed the door, leaving me alone with my pen poised to write an essay titled, "The R-Word: Responsibility."

I wanted to laugh out loud. Mom was right. Usually I *was* oozing with responsibility. But note-passing in science—a major mistake! I wouldn't let Mr. Ross know that I secretly enjoyed having an excuse to write an essay. Writing was my life. Books, too. I mean, if I was going to be stuck on a deserted island, I would definitely take stacks of them, along with lined tablets and sharpened pencils.

By the time Uncle Jack and the cousins showed up, I'd finished my rough draft, fifty words over the 500 limit. *Good . . . room to revise*, I thought as I raced downstairs.

In the living room, Stephie was riding piggyback on her dad. He wore tan dress slacks and a herringbone sports coat. Mark reached up and tried to pull Stephie's hair. When he saw me, Uncle Jack put Stephie down and straightened his striped tie. "The line forms to the right," he said, turning to look outside.

"What line?" squealed Stephie.

He leaned closer to the picture window, pushing the curtains aside. "Guys are flocking to Holly's house. Look, can't you see them?"

Stephie ran over for a peek. I sneaked up behind him and tickled his ribs. "Oh-ho, there," he said,

42

whirling around. "Asking for a tickle session, are you?"

Stephie hollered, "You'll lose, Holly. You will!"

I backed away, giggling. "No thanks, I'll pass."

"Chicken!" Phil shouted, pulling on my arm. "Here, Holly, I'll tell you where he's ticklish."

Uncle Jack pulled out his wallet. "Looks like you're in for a busy evening. Here's payment in advance." *A twenty dollar bill!*

"Uh, that's too much," I said, staring at it.

Uncle Jack acted surprised. "Four kids for four hours? Sounds just right to me."

Goofey wandered into the living room, and Uncle Jack started sneezing. "Stupid allergies," he muttered, taking out a handkerchief to blow his nose. I stuffed the money into my jeans before he could change his mind.

♥   ♥   ♥

After supper, I had all baby-sitting details under control. Carrie and Stephie were playing dolls upstairs, and Mark and Phil were glazed over in front of the Nintendo. I was cleaning the kitchen when the phone rang.

"Hello?" I answered it.

"Is Phil Patterson there?" a tiny voice asked.

"Uh, yes, he is. Who's calling?"

"He knows who it is," *she* said.

I carried the portable phone downstairs to the family room. "Someone wants to talk to you." I handed the phone to ten-year-old Phil.

"Hello?" he said. Silence. Then he yelled, "Aaagh! Get back, it's Elaine Thomas!" He tossed the phone to me.

I stared at Phil while his eyes did a roller coaster number. Mark lay on the floor, laughing hysterically as I quickly pushed the off button.

"What's wrong with Elaine Thomas?" I asked. "She sounds okay to me."

"She's a toidi!" yelled Phil.

"Yeah," shouted Mark.

"Toidi—toidi—toidi—toidi," chanted the boys.

"Sounds like I should flush your mouths out," I said, watching as Phil and his younger brother acted weird. "Okay, okay. What's a toidi?" I asked.

"Idiot spelled backwards," said Phil, cackling.

Never ask, I thought. *Never ask.* I headed back to the kitchen. How did Uncle Jack put up with all this grade-school nonsense? Aunt Marla was in heaven, but her kids needed her down here—learning about toidi and other major stuff. I missed her.

Swishing the kitchen counter clean, I wondered how Aunt Marla would feel if she knew Uncle Jack was dating my mother. Twice in one week!

SIX

The next morning, I beat Andie to Mr. Ross's classroom. "Good morning," I said, standing beside his long desk. "Here's my essay."

Mr. Ross pushed his drooping glasses up his shiny nose.

Without saying a word, he read the entire essay as I stood like a statue, waiting. Slowly, he placed the paper on his desk and removed his glasses. "This essay is unusually well-written, Miss Meredith."

"Thank you," I said.

"I hope you are taking one of Miss Wannamaker's creative writing classes this semester. She impresses me as a teacher who might assist a talented young person such as yourself."

I nodded. "Yes, I love her classes."

"Very well," he said, putting his glasses back on. "Have you had breakfast today?"

"Yes, sir," I said. "I had a fabulous breakfast." Then I added, "My mom's a great cook," in case he had any more notions of contacting the social worker.

Andie arrived, bringing the bustling sounds of the congested hallway in with her. She flashed a smile when she saw me and headed for Mr. Ross. He adjusted his tie, the same boring one he'd worn the whole first month of school.

Andie didn't wait for Mr. Ross to read her essay; she laid it on his desk and left. "What's your rush?" I asked as she zipped past me.

"Gotta do a little spying. On Stan, my man."

"What'll Billy say if he finds out?"

She stopped in the middle of the hall. "Will he even notice?"

"Are you crazy?" I pulled her away from the crush of the crowd. "Billy really likes you."

"Not half as much as I like Stanley J. Patterson."

I wanted to slap some sense into her. "You're wacko if you dump Billy for a schizoid."

"What's *that* mean?" she asked, leaning against the wall.

"Schizoid?" I laughed. "You know, split personality. Sometimes cool, sometimes a real jerk."

"No way, not Stan. He's so-o together," she said, cracking her gum.

"Oh, please," I said. "I oughta know, don't you think?"

She scribbled on her book cover—Andrea Martinez-Patterson. "How's it look?"

"Pathetic."

"What about *this*?" I watched her write Mrs. Stanley J. Patterson in her fanciest handwriting. "Hey, what's the J stand for?"

"Jerk, of course," I said.

"He can't be *that* bad."

"You'll see."

"Worse than Jared?"

"Well, almost."

"I don't believe you," she said, scurrying off.

I trotted down the hall. Then I spotted the number-one jerk of all time—Jared Wilkins—waiting at my locker.

"What do *you* want?" I said, reaching for my combination.

"Nothin' much." He shrugged his shoulders.

"Then what are you doing here?" I said, annoyed.

"Just wondering what you're doing."

"What's it look like?" I stared at him.

"You look upset, Holly. Everything okay?"

"Till *you* showed up it was."

"Holly, listen, I'm not here to cause trouble for you and Danny. It's my own fault he's with you and I'm not." His dancing blue eyes looked surprisingly serious for a change. "I miss you, Holly-Heart."

I could hardly find the numbers on my combination lock. *Where was Danny anyway?* If he were here, like he always was before school, this wouldn't be happening. I looked up to tell Jared to get lost, but he was gone.

♥   ♥   ♥

At lunch, Danny waited for me inside the cafeteria doors. "Ready for volleyball practice today?"

"Can't wait." I grabbed a tray and waited in line. "What's for hot lunch?"

"Some pasta dish," he said, reaching for a tray.

"I'm starved." I saw Mr. Ross peek into the cafeteria. "Guess I better not say that too loud; Mr. Ross might have me hauled off to a foster home."

"That's not funny," Danny said as we moved through the cafeteria line. He reached for a tuna sandwich and an apple. He always ate healthy foods. Apples! *More than one a day keeps the doctor away*, he would say.

"What did you mean about a foster home?" Danny asked, frowning at my choice of pasta and Pepsi.

"Oh, forget it." I walked to a table and sat down.

"Is something wrong?" Danny whispered, setting his tray down beside mine.

"Not really," I said, but it wasn't true. I could still hear Jared's words from this morning. *I miss you, Holly-Heart*. And he'd said it so seriously. Not flirtatiously like always before.

"You seem a little upset, Holly," Danny said before we bowed our heads and he prayed over our lunches. I said amen at the end.

Salting my pasta, I asked where he was this morning before school. "You always show up at my locker first thing."

"Don't use so much salt," he said, criticizing me instead of listening to what I said.

"Where *were* you?" I repeated.

"Oh—Billy and I shot baskets over at the gym." He bit into his tuna sandwich, *lettuce* and all.

"Andie's making a major mistake if she breaks up with Billy. He's so good to her." I twirled noodles around my fork.

Danny looked surprised. "Andie is thinking about breaking up?"

"Yeah," I grumbled. "Didn't I tell you? She's got her eyes on my cousin Stan, but he couldn't care less. He's got a girlfriend back east."

He reached for his milk. "Sounds like you have a problem with Stan."

"It's just that he's nothing like he used to be. Maybe it's Aunt Marla's death, I don't know. But he's turned into a splitzo schizoid."

"A what?"

"A split personality."

"Hey, nobody's perfect," Danny said, chuckling.

His attitude was starting to bug me. I would have thought he'd stick up for Billy—and me! "Whose side are you on, anyway?" I asked.

Danny frowned. "What's this *sides* stuff? Holly, are you feeling okay today?"

I spun around. "That's the second time you've

asked me. Can we just not talk about Stan anymore?"

Danny raised his eyebrows. "If he's the reason you're upset, why don't you talk to him about it? Proverbs says, 'A brother offended is harder to be won than a strong city—'"

"Stan's *not* my brother!" I said, jumping to my feet. "And why do you have to preach to me, Danny? I'm a Christian just like you. First you lecture me about what I eat, and now you tell me what to do with Stan!"

Danny stretched his hand toward me. "I didn't say it to hurt you, Holly. I only want to help."

I pulled away. "That's not how it sounds," I said. "You're trying to run my life." I turned away and ran to the girls' rest room. I was sick of this preachy routine of his.

Scowling in the mirror, I fished for the brush in my purse. I started rearranging my hair, beginning with the bangs. I cringed with every stroke of the brush. How dare Danny Myers use the Bible against me? How dare he treat me like I wasn't a Christian! I bet *he* didn't have a secret prayer list. I bet *he* didn't write in the margins of his devotional! Just because we were boyfriend and girlfriend didn't give him the right to act like this. I marched off to Comp I class in a huff.

Jared was waiting by the door as I hurried to snag my favorite seat . . . beside the window. He followed me into Miss Wannamaker's room. "May I sit here?" he asked, pointing to the desk beside mine. He actually waited until I nodded before he sat down.

"Thanks," he said, like it was a great privilege. His eyes lit up like, uh . . . like Mom's had yesterday when we talked about Uncle Jack.

I swallowed hard. Could it be? Jared Wilkins really and truly in love with me? I pushed the ridiculous thought from my mind as I reached for my three-ring binder.

"Dear class," Miss Wannamaker said like in a letter. It was her way, everyday. "Today we shall discuss the proper outlining procedures for research papers."

I found the yellow tab marking the "Comp. I" section in my binder and set out to take the best notes ever. After her lecture, Miss W gave us twenty minutes to begin the assignment—an 800-word essay or short story using any aspect of a metamorphosis, human or otherwise. It was due in two weeks.

First, I looked up metamorphosis in Webster's dictionary. It meant, "A complete change of a substance, structure, or shape."

Hmm, what to write about? Staring out the window, I watched as golden aspen leaves shimmered in the autumn breeze. A transformation of color!

My eyes wandered to the top of Copper Mountain. Years before, men had sliced a path through the tree-covered slopes, transforming the mountain into a skier's paradise. Nope, I wouldn't write a nature essay. Not this time.

I let my eyes wander slightly to my left. There sat Jared, his pen racing across the blank page. *What if?* I thought. What if I let my imagination run wild? What if I transformed Jared Wilkins into a polite, trustworthy, *true* love—a magical metamorphosis—on paper only!

Delighted with my idea, I set to work, using Jared's name just to help me relate more closely to the final fictitious character. I would change names later, of course.

Finishing the first paragraph, I set my pen down and sneaked a glance at Jared. I grinned at the thought of transforming him. The idea excited me more than I cared to admit!

SEVEN

It was a week later—two days before Carrie's surprise birthday party. When I arrived at school, Andie was waiting for me in the main hall, near the front doors. "Where've you been?" she said, biting her nails. "I thought you were sick or something. I even looked in your locker and—"

"You opened my locker?" I said, moving through the crowd of kids in the hall, hoping she hadn't snooped *too* much.

"I oughta know your combination by now, don't you think?" She stayed close to the wall to avoid mad scramblers headed for lockers, homerooms, you-name-it.

"Have you been in my locker before?" I asked, feeling uneasy, wondering if she'd discovered my writing assignment. It was nearly finished, and no way did I want *anyone* but Miss Wannamaker to see the finished product!

She looked at me, surprised. "Well, we *are* best friends."

"I know, Andie. It's no big deal," I said, playing it down in case she picked up on my concern and suspected something. Still, I dashed to my locker.

It was hanging open!

"Andie, you left my locker open!"

"I did?"

"You just said you opened it!" I hoped she was the *only* one snooping around. There was top secret stuff in there.

"Sorry," Andie said. "Guess I was just in a hurry to catch up with you."

I shook my head, fuming at her. "There's no excuse for irresponsibility," I muttered, reaching for my three-ring binder. I flipped it to the yellow tab marked "Comp I" and noticed two pages were out of order. Maybe I had mixed them up myself. I grabbed my science book and closed my locker. "Why were you looking for me before?"

"It's about Stan Patterson," she said, starry-eyed.

I should've known! Between Andie and Kayla I almost wished Uncle Jack and my cousins had stayed in Pennsylvania. Well, not really—then Mom wouldn't be having fun going on dates with Uncle Jack . . . and I wouldn't be ready for a new tax bracket!

"Just tell me one thing," Andie continued. "Is he coming with the youth group to the ice cream social on Saturday?" She grabbed my arm. "Because if he is, I need a new outfit."

"You do not," I said. "Besides, he doesn't even know about it. Uncle Jack's been trying out different churches since they moved here."

"Can't *you* invite Stan for me?" she pleaded.

"I could, but I won't," I said, heading for science.

"But he's so adorable with that gorgeous blond hair and those blue eyes," she said. "Please?"

"He's not *that* adorable." I opened the door to the stairwell. There stood Kayla. "Hi," I said, brushing past her on my way to first period. She'd been driving me crazy, too, with her phone calls every single night of my life since our chat in front of the Soda Straw last week.

"Wait! Holly!" Kayla called, running up the stairs after me. "Will you give this to Stan for me?" She held out an envelope, sealed and addressed with his name only.

"Why me?" I stared at it; a hint of sweet perfume rose up out of the paper.

Andie pushed past me, scowling at Kayla. "Leave Stan alone . . . he's mine!" The love note fell to the steps.

"Ex-cu-se me!" I scurried up the steps, leaving Andie and Kayla alone with their misery.

After school—volleyball! Danny met me as usual. I was hesitant to see him. The past week had been very up and down between us. If it wasn't his health kick, it was his concern over my relationship with Stan. Then there was the constant quoting from Scripture. Our relationship was on the brink of break-up, and nothing I could say seemed to make a difference. He was even opposed to my reading so many mysteries. *Might not be good for you, all that detective stuff,* he'd said at lunch yesterday.

More than ever, I wondered what I'd seen in him in the first place. "How's the team?" he asked, interrupting my thoughts.

"The team's fine. But Stan's still a pain," I said, nodding toward my cousin, who was writing on his clipboard like some hotshot.

"Why? What's he doing?" Danny asked.

"Just watch," I said. As I hurried to take my spot on the court, I nearly plowed into Jared, who appeared out of nowhere.

Our first serve flew over the net. It came back high and short so I spiked the ball, giving us a point.

Later, when I was up to serve, Stan blew his whistle at me. "Watch your right leg, Holly," he yelled.

I looked down. I was nowhere near the boundary line! Taking a tiny step backward, I served.

Net ball! It was Stan's fault for picking on me. A few minutes later he blew his whistle at me again. "Carrying!" he shouted. He pointed at the other side. "Your serve."

I turned to Miss Tucker, who sat on the bench. "Coach?" She nodded her head, agreeing with Stan.

Just then Paula Miller, Kayla's twin, showed up.

She sat on the front row of the bleachers, her eyes glued to Jared, who stood on the other side of the gym.

Kayla served next. We volleyed back and forth three times before I set it up for Amy-Liz, who spiked it over. When it came back low, I stretched to reach under the ball but fell out of bounds trying.

Stan blew his whistle while I lay sprawled on the floor. I wanted to wrap his precious whistle around his neck.

Danny came over. "You okay?"

"See what I mean?" I whispered to him, getting up.

"It *does* seem like he's singling you out."

"It's not fair. Stan's picking on me for no reason."

Folding his arms, Danny said, " 'Be at peace with each other,' Mark 9:50 says."

I glared at him. He was preaching again, and it *really* bugged me.

Jared wandered over, eyeing Stan. "What's he think he's doing?"

I shrugged, feeling strange with all this attention. It was almost like a story I'd written called, "Love Times Two," except now instead of two girls chasing one boy, it was Danny and Jared after me!

Stan blew his whistle again. "Take your position, Holly," he called.

"You better quit picking on me," I said right in his face.

Kayla pointed to the spot next to her. "Play here, Holly. Please?"

"Oh no, you don't. If you want info about Stan, ask him yourself."

"Hol-ly," she whined.

I moved to another spot, away from the schizoid-crazy female. Danny sat on the sidelines, watching Stan like a hawk. Jared sat high in the bleachers, cheering every shot I made. Kayla kept looking at me, even though I tried my best to ignore her. And Paula? She looked lovesick over Jared.

At last, practice was over. Kayla sauntered over to Danny, probably as an excuse to get close to Stan. But Danny ignored her, peering over Stan's shoulder, studying his clipboard. I should've been thrilled to have a guy looking out for me like that, but the real excitement was coming from high in the bleachers. I could feel Jared's eyes on me, even though I refused to satisfy him with a glance.

I dashed to the locker room, hoping to escape a lecture from Stan. And to get away from Danny, who seemed to have a Scripture for everything lately. Taking my time, I dragged out my shower and hid in the locker room until I was sure Stan and Danny were gone.

Sneaking past the doors leading to the gym, I headed for the hall to my locker. The door creaked open and I heard my name. It was Stan. The whistle still hung from his neck as he called to me.

"What do *you* want?" I growled.

"Look," he said, catching up with me. "I don't know what's bugging you, cuz, but—"

"Me? Why don't *you* get rid of that stupid whistle for starters!"

He laughed. "You think you're so hot, Holly, but you're not as good as you think you are."

"I'd play better if you weren't breathing down my neck every second." I flung my hair off my shoulder.

"Blame it on me, if you want. I'm just doing what I do best."

"Right—making a jerk of yourself, bossing people around."

"So *that's* it. You can't handle your cousin calling the shots." He put his hand on his hip.

I clenched my fist. "This was *my* school first!"

"Well, it's my school now." His lips curled into a sickening smile.

"You really have an attitude problem," I said, tapping my toe as hard as I could.

He laughed under his breath. "So . . . we're stuck in the same school. What's the big deal?"

"Yeah," I mumbled, looking away. "Stuck, all right."

"Listen, Holly." He sounded serious. "I don't like this thing between my dad and your mom any more than you do."

I couldn't believe my ears!

"You're crazy, Stan! Their dating has nothing to do with us." I stared him down.

"Well, your *boyfriend* thinks so."

"Danny?" I was shocked.

"He thinks you're mad at me because my dad's dating your mom."

"Well, he's wrong," I said, turning to go. "I like Uncle Jack taking Mom out. She's having fun for a change. And Danny has no right to say anything about it." I shifted my gym bag to my right shoulder.

"Whatever," Stan said, shoving open the gym door with a mighty push as he left.

So much for confiding in Danny! Be at peace with each other, huh? Well, Danny better learn to practice what he preaches instead of stirring up trouble!

I ran down the hall, opened my locker, and buried my head inside. It was a mess in here! Usually my things were super organized, but my volleyball schedule was making neatness impossible. I pulled everything out of my locker and sat on the floor, sorting . . . and letting the anger pour out.

Soon I heard footsteps . . . coming closer. I spun around expecting to see Stan again.

It was Jared.

"Need help?" he asked.

"What are you doing here?" I flipped through my assignment book.

"Waiting to see you." His smooth voice reminded me of last year when I first met him.

"Danny wouldn't like it," I said, avoiding his eyes.

"He's gone, Holly. I saw him leave thirty minutes ago."

The way he said that made me curious. "Did he say anything when he left?"

"Just that he thought you needed space to work things out with Stan." He sat on the floor, leaning against Andie's locker.

"There he goes second-guessing me again. Some nerve after he interferes with me and my cousin." I made a pile of papers on the floor.

Jared picked up my books. "Wish I could help."

"It's no use," I said, organizing everything inside my locker. "I have to work it out myself."

"Okay, but remember—I'm here if you need me."

I wanted to cover my ears and run away from him. "Please, not now, Jared. Don't do this, okay?"

"Just tell me one thing, Holly, and I'll leave," he said, his face looking truly serious. "If I can prove that I've changed, will you give me a second chance?" He stood tall, almost stiff . . . waiting.

Words escaped me as I stared in disbelief at Jared. Handsome, sweet-talking Jared.

He turned to go. "Think about it, Holly. Maybe I'll see you at the Soda Straw on Saturday."

I could only nod as he turned and walked away. Strange . . . this was the very thing I'd dreamed up for my creative writing assignment. But *could* Jared change? And how would Danny feel if I dumped him for Jared, my first love?

EIGHT

At home, Carrie's announcement took my mind off Jared's words. "There's a huge envelope in the mail for you," she said the minute I stepped in the door.

"There is?" I followed her to the kitchen. On the desk was a pile of letters waiting to be opened. I picked up a manila envelope, eyeing the return address. Yes! What I'd been waiting for.

Reaching for a sharp knife from the wooden wall rack, I carefully sliced it open. Inside, a typewritten letter was attached to my story, "Love Times Two."

"What is it?" Carrie asked, leaning on my arm.

"It's from Marty Leigh, the editor of *Sealed With A Kiss*, a new teen magazine."

"Can I see it?"

"Let me read it first." I held the embossed stationery, reading every word before handing it to Carrie. Enclosed was a copy of my story with red markings in the margin. I scanned the manuscript. Marty Leigh had written suggestions for revisions. And if I worked hard, I could whip my story into shape for the very first issue.

"Wow! Twenty-five bucks. You're gonna be rich!" Carrie said, reading the letter.

"That's not rich. I make almost that much in one evening baby-sitting for our cousins." I slid the letter and story back into the envelope. "Where's Mom?"

"Buying stuff for my birthday. What are *you* getting me with all your money?"

"It's a secret." I scampered off to my room, carrying the cordless phone with me.

"Holly!" Carrie bounded up the steps after me. "Give me one little hint."

"I haven't bought it yet," I answered absently, pulling my journal out of its usual place.

"Phooey," Carrie said, trudging out of my room and back downstairs.

I closed the door, hopped up onto my window seat, and began writing. *Thursday, September 30th: The best thing about today came in the mail. I might become published this year! The worst thing that happened was my fight with Stan after volleyball practice. He's turning into a total jerk. I can't begin to imagine what Andie or Kayla see in him. Maybe it's his looks, but blue-eyed blonds are no big deal.*

Jared's acting strange. Not his usual flirty-strange—

something's different. He wants a second chance, but I don't think I can trust him. And then there's Danny— he's getting more and more preachy every day. Besides, he said stuff about Mom and Uncle Jack dating to Stan. It really got me mad! Sometimes I think we were better off just friends.

Ding-dong! The doorbell.

"Carrie, look out the window before you answer it," I called down the steps.

"It's Andie. Should I let her in?"

"Of course, silly." I sat down on the top step waiting for my best friend.

She wore dark green leggings and an oversized sweater. "Hi! What's up?" she asked, taking the steps two at a time.

"You'll never believe it," I said, leading the way to my room.

"Try me." She closed the door behind us.

I poured out my woes, first about Stan, then about Jared's plea for a second chance. Andie's eyes grew wider with each new detail. "I can't believe Stan would treat you that way," she said finally. "He's just so, so wonderful."

"Believe it, it's true." I leaned against the pillows piled up on my bed.

"Now Jared's another story. You can't believe him, Holly, not for a single minute. In fact, I guarantee he's the same smooth-talking two-timer he ever was!"

"What if for some reason he really wants to change?"

Andie looked shocked. "I can't believe you just said that, Holly! You've really lost it."

Our eyes locked for an instant, then I turned away.

"Holly?" she said, touching my arm. "You still like Jared, don't you?"

"Maybe a little. I don't know."

"He hurt you once; he'll do it again." She slid over beside me. "Besides, what would make him want to change?"

I toyed with telling her about my story assignment—about the transformation of Jared Wilkins, only not using his name. But would she let me live it down?

"You're better off with Danny," she said. "Even though he's too, too much sometimes. Just because he remembers Bible verses is no excuse for *using* them on his friends. He told me the other day that I should read Proverbs 21:23. When I went home and looked it up, I couldn't believe it."

"What?"

"Are you ready for this? 'He who guards his mouth and his tongue keeps himself from calamity.' Hey, why didn't he just come right out and say I talk too much?"

I giggled.

"One thing, though, I'll probably never forget that verse. So I guess if you look hard enough, Danny's not so bad."

"Maybe, but it seems like Danny and I got along better before. Now he keeps telling me what to do.

And it really bugs me." I scooted off the bed, picking up my three-ring binder off the floor.

"*Now* what are you doing?" Andie asked.

"If you promise not to try to change my mind, I'll let you in on a secret."

She pulled up her socks. "I knew it! I just knew those little wheels were turnin' inside that brain of yours. Holly Meredith, you're up to no good!"

"Here's my plan. Since Jared seems positively sincere about wanting me back—even said he'd prove that he's changed—I've come up with the perfect plan."

Andie leaned forward, all ears. "Like what?"

"A test."

"What kind of test?"

"A test designed to analyze his behavior." I turned to my outline. "Here, look at this."

"Whoa, Holly, you're not kidding, are you? That's one hefty checklist. He'll never make it, you know."

"There's more. I want you to help me."

"Me? How?"

"By being your charming self. You know, flirt with him, ask him to sit with you at youth meetings, call him up. Stuff like that."

"He'll think you put me up to it, Holly. It'll never work."

"Maybe it will, maybe it won't. But it's worth a try. Please, Andie?"

She twisted a curl around her finger. "If I *do* cooperate with your little scheme, what will you do for me?"

"I should've known." I leaped to my closet. "Choose anything. You can wear it for as long as you want."

"Good try, Holly, but you've overlooked one tiny detail."

"Oh?" I said, playing innocent.

"You're a size 3 and I'm a size, uh . . . bigger."

"What about jewelry, books, teddy bears?"

"We *already* traded our favorite bears, remember?" she said, still playing my game.

"So." I turned to the mirror. "What is it you want?" I brushed my hair, knowing exactly what she'd say.

"Stan, your cousin. Can you deliver him to me?"

"You want him baked, boiled, or fried?" I faced her. "After everything you know about my cousin, you're still mushy over him?"

"What about you and your Jared fixation? I see a parallel. And you can't say one word about it, because in my opinion, you're doing worse. Much worse."

She had a point. I knew Stan was wrong for her, and she felt the same about Jared. I sighed. "Who knows if I can talk Stan into anything right now. We're not exactly on the best terms."

Andie leaped off my bed. "I've got it! Invite him to the ice cream social. Tell him you want to introduce him to all the kids at your church. When it comes to tables, make sure Stan sits across from you and Danny. Then leave the rest to me. Okay?"

No way would Stan attend a social with *my* church group.

Andie smiled up into my face. "You don't want to be stuck with Danny all year, now do you?"

I pulled on my braid. It wouldn't be easy getting Stan to show up on Saturday, but in order to get Andie's help with Jared's scrutiny test, I had to. "Okay, it's a deal," I said. "Here, let's sign a secret pact." I reached for my journal, found today's entry, and neatly printed the plan.

At the bottom of the page, Andie scribbled her name and the date. I wrote my name in my best cursive, under hers. It was a deal.

NINE

The minute Andie disappeared, I called Stan.

"Patterson Consulting." It was Uncle Jack.

"Hi, it's Holly. Is Stan home?"

"Hi, kiddo. Let's see if I can scrounge him up for you."

Uncle Jack was like that. Upbeat and . . . cool. Couldn't remember ever seeing him grump around. Even when Aunt Marla died, he was sad, not crabby.

He was back. "Stan says he's busy. Tried to hogtie him and drag him over here, but couldn't get him tied up to haul."

I giggled. "So, Stan won't talk to me."

"Don't take it seriously, cutie. Stan's in blue funk."

"Blue funk?"

"Ever been there?" he asked with a chuckle.

"He's like . . . depressed, is that it?"

"Come to think of it, depressed is a step up from blue funk."

I took a deep breath. "Well, I can't really blame him. It's partly my fault." I remembered the dumb stuff we'd said to each other after school.

"Is there a message I can zap him with?"

"Tell him my youth group's having an ice cream social at the Soda Straw this Saturday at two-thirty. And . . . I wanted to invite him."

"Sounds delicious," Uncle Jack said. "Any *girls* Stan knows?"

"Lots of them," I said, laughing.

"I'll tell him. That oughta make some points."

"Thanks," I said, feeling weird about Uncle Jack being in the middle of my plan.

"It may be just the thing he needs right now. You know, to bring him back from blue funk." I didn't know what *that* meant, but I said good-bye anyway and hung up.

After school on Friday, we had a long volleyball practice beginning with three laps around the gym. Miss Tucker—not Stan—called the shots today, carrying the clipboard around, smoothing her short dark hair, and blowing the whistle. Stan kept score while Kayla flashed her sugar-wide smile at him every few minutes. It was disgusting.

Stan looked positively bummed out, like he'd lost his best friend. After practice, he called me over to the bench.

"Hey, cuz, what's this about Saturday?"

"Just an ice cream bash with a bunch of kids," I said coolly, secretly hoping he was interested.

"Yeah?" he said.

"Yeah."

"I'll be there." He wore a kind, almost pained expression. What could be wrong? I had more sense than to ask. Didn't want to spoil this amazing breakthrough.

"Okay, see ya." I hurried to the locker room, changed clothes without showering, and raced home to call Andie.

♥   ♥   ♥

Saturday morning—Carrie's birthday! Uncle Jack showed up before she finished breakfast. He winked at me as he and Stephanie escorted the birthday girl out of the house.

As soon as they backed out of the driveway, Mom scurried around, opening kitchen cupboards, pulling out party supplies. "Wanna help me decorate the dining room?"

"Perfect," I said, reaching for the apricot-colored rolls of crepe paper lined up on the kitchen bar. Decorating for parties was one of my favorite things. I would transform the dining room into a magical maze of apricot clouds whispering against the ceiling-sky. Balloons would shimmy beneath the crepe paper canopy and dance to the birthday song.

I slid a chair close to the corner and went to work. "Wish I could see Carrie's face when she gets home."

"She'll be surprised all right," Mom said from the kitchen.

I twisted and looped until the dining room had disappeared. In its place was a merry party land, fit for a nine-year-old princess. Taking a giant breath, I began blowing up balloons.

Mom came in just then, gazing at my creation. "It's wonderful, Holly. You've outdone yourself again."

My cheeks burned from balloon blowing. I stopped to catch my breath. "Sure could use Stan's help. He's the best balloon blower-upper I know."

Mom straightened the tablecloth. "He may not be the best help now. His girlfriend back east broke up with him."

No wonder he looked so depressed yesterday. But what fabulous timing! Andie would be delirious with the news. "That's too bad," I said, feeling a tiny bit sorry for my schizoid cousin.

"Maybe you could introduce him to some of the girls in your youth group." Mom had a twinkle in her eye. "It would be nice if Stan had a church home, uh, with us, you know."

I knew what she was getting at. "And it would be nice if Uncle Jack went to the same church as we do, right, Mom?"

She blushed and headed into the kitchen to bake Carrie's birthday cake.

At two-thirty, the Soda Straw was packed with ice cream freaks. Danny was prompt as usual. He waved to me from the booth in the corner. I slid into the seat across from him. He looked puzzled, probably about the seating arrangement I'd chosen. "Hi" was all he said.

I picked up a menu and explained. "We need to save space for my cousin Stan. He said he was coming."

"Okay with me," Danny said. "Did you and Stan patch things up?"

"Not really. Just trying to befriend the new kid on the block." I snickered at the way it sounded. It was much more than that.

Kayla and Paula arrived wearing look-alike jump suits. Carrot-orange . . . like two-legged vegetables. Even the identical ponytails, pulled off to the side, stuck out like the tassels of homegrown carrots! Next came Amy-Liz with her friends Shauna and Joy. Billy Hill and Jared arrived together, followed by Stan and a bunch of others. Where was Andie?

I excused myself and rushed over to Stan. Had to keep my part of the pact, and in order to do it, Stan had to sit with Danny and me at our booth.

"Wanna sit with us?" I asked, pointing at Danny, who sat in the corner behind the jukebox.

Stan nodded as we passed a table of girls, and Kayla—who now looked more like a smiley pumpkin than a boring carrot. It was that sugar-sweet grin of hers, again.

Jared didn't flirt—only smiled—when I swept past him. In a strange sort of way, I missed his winks.

When I got back to our table, the waitress showed up and we ordered. A strawberry sundae, with three scoops of ice cream for me, a root beer float for Danny, and for Stan, who sat across the table from us, a banana split.

Danny and Stan began talking immediately, discussing favorite sports figures. "Wanna borrow my book on Dravecky?" Danny asked him.

"Sure would," Stan said. "Thanks."

Soon our waitress brought the desserts. I looked at my watch. Two forty-five! What was taking Andie so long? Dipping into the giant sundae in front of me, I fumed. This wasn't like her. Where *was* she?

Spooning up my ice cream, I retreated into strawberry heaven. "Nothing like it," I muttered, as Danny stared.

"You're going to eat *all* that?" he said.

I snickered. "Just watch."

Stan leaned forward on his elbows. "You ain't seen nothin' yet. She eats ice cream like it's rare and endangered."

Danny kept staring. "You'll get sick, Holly. I wish you'd go easy."

I didn't like how that sounded. I wanted to tell him to mind his own business.

Pastor Rob wandered over. "Hi," he said, shaking hands with Stan. "You a friend of Holly's?"

"We're cousins," Stan said, introducing himself.

I noticed Kayla creeping up behind our youth

74

pastor. She'd locked her cat eyes on Stan, watching his every move.

Ding-a-ding-a-ling!

I turned to see Andie coming in the door, pushing a double-wide twin stroller. All heads turned as my best friend made her grand entrance with her baby brothers dressed in matching Winnie the Pooh outfits.

"Hi, Holly," she said, heading for our table. She parked the stroller in the aisle. Girls came from all directions, stumbling over each other to get to Jon and Chris. "Help yourself," she said, handing Jon to Shauna.

Chris whimpered when he spied my sundae. "Here, baby brother, you go to Auntie Holly," Andie said, picking him up and planting him on my lap. The girls clapped as I gave him a taste of my ice cream.

"Smart kid," Stan said with a grin.

But Danny looked worried. "Shouldn't he go easy on sweets?"

"Lighten up," I whispered. "Two-year-olds can eat most anything."

Shauna quickly brought Jon back to Andie. He must've seen me feeding his brother, because he let out a wail as Andie took him. "It's okay, buddy, you can share some of mine," Andie said. Then she began to work her magic on Stan. She rocked Jon from side to side, standing beside our table, talking babytalk to her brothers, chatting with Stan and Danny and me. I almost asked her to sit with us, but remembered she wanted to handle things *her* way.

The waitress came back with her order pad. "Can I get you anything else here?" she asked.

"Yes, please." Andie leaned over with Jon in her arms and reached for the menu on the table. "Could you hold him a sec?" she asked Stan.

"Fork him over," Stan said, sliding up against the wall to let Andie in the booth beside him!

Amazing! I thought, pushing the gooshy remains of my sundae aside.

"Anyone else?" the waitress asked.

"Yes, may I please have an order of fries?"

Danny stared at me, obviously shocked, as the waitress nodded and cleared away my dish.

"Like I said," Stan said. "You ain't seen nothin' yet!" Little Jon pulled on the pocket of his shirt with sloppy wet fingers. It didn't faze Stan one bit.

"You're really good with kids," Andie said.

Stan nodded and smiled, then made funny faces to make Jon laugh.

Kayla swaggered over to our table. "Looks like you could use some help here." She reached for Chris, who was bouncing and chattering on my lap. Then she stood there with him, smiling at Stan, who was too busy with Jon to notice. Soon she left, taking chubby Chris back to her table, where her sister and three other girls sat.

The waitress came back with my fries. I salted them and poured catsup off to the side.

Danny cleared his throat. "Any idea what Proverbs 23:20–21 says?"

"Let me guess. Something about eating too much?" I giggled when Andie raised her eyebrows.

"Tell her," Stan said, egging him on. "Tell her good."

Danny began to recite, " 'Do not join those who drink too much wine or gorge themselves on meat, for drunkards and gluttons become poor, and drowsiness clothes them in rags.' "

Andie clapped. I boiled. This wasn't funny.

The other kids were settled at tables all around the restaurant oblivious to what was happening. Slowly, I turned to face Danny. "Do you have any idea how high and mighty these remarks make you look?"

"They're God's words, not mine," Danny said solemnly, still frowning at my french fries.

"Okay, then, what about *this* verse? First Corinthians 10:31: 'Whether you eat or drink or whatever you do, do it all for the glory of God.' "

"Bravo!" Andie said.

I glared at her. "Stay out of this, Andie."

Her eyes widened as I took another bite.

Stan, embarrassed, excused himself, sliding out of the booth with little Jon. Andie moved out to make room for him. She shot me a weird look and helped Stan buckle Jon into the stroller.

"Let's grab some space," Stan said, heading away from us, stroller and all.

"Just great, Danny," I said. "Look what you've done. My cousin shows up for the first time at our group and you go and scare him off."

"Doesn't look like he's too scared to me."

I turned to see Stan and Andie settling in at a quiet corner booth across the room. Looked like Andie was doing just fine without me! Mr. Macho Man pushed the stroller back and forth with his foot, while Andie chattered away.

Talk about split personality. Maybe now Andie would see what I meant about Stan. How could a guy sneer at his cousin and carry on with two-years-olds all in the same day?

Disgusted, I turned toward my french fries. "Well, never mind about them, Danny," I said. "*We* aren't working out."

"We aren't?" Danny pushed his glass away and leaned on his elbow, frowning at me. "You're upset again, is that it?"

"Do I have to spell it out?" I said, standing up.

Danny leaned back against the red vinyl seat, folding his arms. *Oh, fabulous*, I thought. *He has to think this one through!*

I reached for my purse and grabbed my windbreaker. "Good-bye, Danny," I said, heading for the door. Under my breath, I said, "Good-bye forever."

TEN

I stomped down the sidewalk and headed across the street toward the park, inhaling the brisk mountain air. Breaking up with Danny wasn't as hard as I'd thought it would be. In fact, I hadn't even planned on doing it—it just happened! And I didn't feel one bit sorry.

When I spotted the swing sets in the park, I began to run. I needed to put some distance between me and that bossy Danny Myers.

The park buzzed with the sounds of little kids. Some were hanging upside-down on the monkey bars, others were swinging higher than high, and three girls sat digging in the sandbox. Finding my favorite wooden bench near a clump of aspen trees, I sat down to think. Thinking doesn't always solve everything, but it helps. Not as much as praying though.

The sun felt warm on my back, so I unzipped my jacket. Leaning back, I observed a giant cloud formation. A two-headed monster with floppy ears and a bushy mustache grinned down at me. Slowly . . . slowly his grin faded and a triple-decker strawberry sundae took its place.

Ice cream!

I sat up, hungry for the ice cream and french fries I'd left behind. Then I snickered. Danny was stuck with the bill, and it served him right for hounding me about my food cravings. Phooey on him! Somehow I couldn't picture *Jared* acting that way.

Shoving thoughts of Danny out of my mind, I pulled a small tablet out of my purse and began writing my list from memory.

Jared must observe all of the following until Thanksgiving Day.

1. No flirting.
2. No talking to girls.
3. Must not accept phone calls from girls.
4. Must not accept letters, notes, or cards from girls.
5. Must not . . .

I felt someone watching me. Looking up, I jumped. Jared!

He was gazing at me intently, holding my container of french fries. "Still hungry?"

I reached for it, smiling. "Thanks, Jared." It had

been ages since I'd said anything nice to this hunk of humanity.

"No problem." He was still standing behind me, his brown hair picking up highlights from the sun.

"Did you see what happened with Danny and me back there?" I took a french fry.

"It was pretty obvious, don't you think?"

"How'd you know I'd be here?" I asked.

"I pay close attention to details." He winked. Then he grabbed my tablet off the bench!

"Jared!" I leaped off the bench and reached for the tablet. "That's private!"

But he twisted away, and before I could stop him, he had opened it!

"Some list you've got going," he said flirtatiously.

"It's none of your business!" I said.

"Does this mean I get the second chance we talked about?" he asked, holding the tablet high over his head.

"*We* didn't talk about any such thing."

"You're right, Holly. It was my idea." He handed the tablet back to me, leaning on the back of the bench. "But you won't be sorry if you give me a second chance, not for a second."

"I haven't promised anything." I stepped back, secretly admiring him.

"But you are thinking about it, aren't you?" He was pushing the second chance idea hard. But why?

"Just look at the list again." I opened the tablet

and handed it to him. "I made it impossible, as you can see."

"Whatever it takes," he said, scanning the page then shifting his gaze to me. A smile crept across his face.

"What's this *really* about, Jared?" I set the french fries aside. "Why do you want to prove you're not a flirt anymore?"

"The truth?"

I nodded, waiting for his answer.

His blue eyes grew sober. "There's only one reason." He took a deep breath. "I *miss* you, Holly. I want you to go out with me."

My heart beat wildly. What's a girl to do? The best-looking guy in the entire universe declares his feelings and what do I do? Come that close to believing him!

I blew my bangs and mustered up enough courage to spell out my plan. "Okay, here's the deal," I said, taking the tablet back. "I make a list of do's and don't's . . ." I needed a name for the plan—fast! So I chose the exact same name I'd used in my story. "Uh, we'll call it the Scrutiny Test to Analyze Nascence. You sign on the dotted line and I watch and wait."

"Nascence?" he said, coming around and sitting in the grass in front of me. *"That's* a word?"

"Nascence is birth or growth . . . maturity. Like when a Christian reads the Bible and talks to the Lord every day. Change happens—like a metamorphosis."

"Now you sound like Danny," he said.

I gasped. "I do?"

Jared shook his head. "Just joking." Then he said, "Where do you get these words, Holly?"

"I read a lot. Sometimes even the dictionary."

"The dictionary?"

"When I'm bored."

Jared stretched his arms over his head, studying me. At least he wasn't laughing. Not yet. "And what if I pass this Scrutiny Test to Analyze the Nascence of Jared Wilkins, what then?"

"What do you mean?" I said, knowing exactly what he was getting at.

"Will you go out with me then?"

"There's *no way* you'll pass."

He leaned forward, looking more thoughtful than ever. "And if I do?"

"I can't promise anything, Jared." It sounded heartless, but this boy had a flirting reputation that didn't quit. No way would it disappear in two months . . . or at all!

He reached over and picked up the french fry dish. "Guess I better return this." He stood up, brushing the grass from his faded jeans. "So when do we start this test of yours?"

"Tomorrow," I said, standing up. "And to keep it a secret, let's use the code word S.T.A.N.—for Scrutiny Test to Analyze Nascence—get it? It'll be perfect at school. Kids will just think we're talking about my cousin." It might even drive Stan Patterson crazy if he overheard us talking about S.T.A.N. Who knows, it might irritate that stupid whistle off his neck! It was the perfect code word.

"Whatever the writer says," Jared replied.

"I'll get right to work on it." Then I remembered the rewrite on "Love Times Two." "Wait! I can't have S.T.A.N. ready by tomorrow."

"Why not?" He looked positively crushed as he fell in step with me, heading for the street.

I told him about the new teen magazine, *Sealed With A Kiss*. "The first issue comes out next month. Romance stories for girls only."

"Who's the editor?"

"Marty Leigh, the best mystery writer of all time."

"I've heard of her. Where's her magazine published?"

I told him, wondering why he was so interested.

"I have to read your story when it comes out," he said. "Now, how soon can we start S.T.A.N.?"

"Monday," I said. "That'll give me the rest of the weekend to plan it."

We were coming up on the Soda Straw. I hung back when Paula and Kayla—the jumpsuited wonders—slinked down the steps waiting for Amy-Liz and her friends. Then I spotted Danny and Billy leaving together. "Guess you'd better go in without me," I said.

"Yeah, I see what you mean," Jared said, slowing his pace.

"Besides," I added, "this could be your last chance to flirt before S.T.A.N. starts."

Jared smiled the dearest smile ever. "Test or no test, those days are over now, Holly. You'll see."

I couldn't believe my ears! His words sounded

like something straight out of my story assignment for Miss W's comp class!

My heart sank as he ran across the street to the Soda Straw. I missed him already. Too bad. There was no chance this side of the Continental Divide that deep down the two-timing Jared Wilkins could ever *truly* reform.

I ran to catch the city bus, slipping into a seat on the side facing the Soda Straw—hoping for one last glance of Jared.

He dashed up the walkway and toward the door . . . without so much as a fleeting look at Paula Miller or any other girl!

ELEVEN

I hopped off the bus a block away from Explore Bookstore. Carrie's birthday party was probably going strong about now. I could almost hear the kids singing "Happy birthday to you!"

Soft music greeted me as I opened the door to my favorite bookstore—busy as usual. I headed straight to the stationery section. A diary—the perfect birthday gift for my sister. Now that she was nine, she needed to be recording the events of her life.

An array of diaries and journals of all styles, colors, and sizes were lined up on the shelf. Clothbound ones with pink polka-dot hearts and others wearing jazzy stripes. There were five-year diaries with teeny-tiny locks and keys no bigger than a fat toothpick, and flowery ones with famous sayings inside. I stepped closer, opening the one with the tiny lock and key.

Behind me, I heard familiar voices. Turning, I noticed the Miller twins coming into the store. They saw me, too. I waved, but really wished they'd leave me alone.

My wish didn't work. Here they came, all smiles—those sugary ones. Kayla spoke first. "Hi, Holly. Buying a diary?"

"For my little sister," I said, half ignoring her.

"I need to talk to you." She moved closer. "Is Andie going out with Stan?"

I shrugged. "Don't know."

"They sat together at the Soda Straw, playing with Andie's baby brothers for the longest time," she said, prying for answers.

"I honestly don't know, Kayla," I said, inspecting a red five-year diary.

Paula spoke up. "What about Danny Myers?"

"What about him?" I kept my eyes on the row of diaries.

"Are you still going out with him?"

"What do *you* think?" I turned to see two sets of made-up brown eyes. Exactly alike.

"Andie said you and Danny had a fight," Paula continued. "And you called it quits and that Jared ran off after you."

"People come and people go," I said flippantly. *How nosy can you get?*

It was Kayla's turn. "Paula likes Jared, you know." She glanced at her twin, giggling.

"Really?" I said coolly, wondering why Paula

couldn't speak for herself. It made me feel weird seeing her all batty-eyed over Jared, while I planned a scrutiny test to prove he was still a jerk.

Wait a minute! A brilliant idea struck. Paula Miller could be prime Jared-bait—the perfect person to assist me with the S.T.A.N. test!

"Jared's a lonely guy these days. Maybe you could help cheer him up, Paula," I said.

She was all ears. "What's wrong?"

"Oh, nothing's really *wrong*, he's just gotten lousy press from the girls in this town. A rumor's been going around about him being a smooth-talking two-timer, or . . . something like that."

Paula's eyes lit up. "Yeah, I know. Last spring when we first came to Dressel Hills, Andie warned us about him. She said he was rotten." She batted her mascara-laden lashes. "But he seems nice to me."

"Why don't you give him a call sometime soon?" I picked up the pink polka-dot diary.

"You two friends?" Paula asked.

"Jared and I go way back." I pulled out a scrap of paper and wrote down his phone number. "Here, call him tonight."

Her eyes sparkled and the famous smile emerged. "Thanks, I will!"

I oughta thank her! I thought, giddy all over.

Then Kayla stepped forward like she was going to corner me. "What about Stan? Can you find out if he's going to ask Andie out?"

"Me?" I said, taking a step backward.

"You're his cousin. Please?" She was whining

again. This was too much. Were my eyes playing tricks on me or what? The orange jumpsuits were closing in—making me jumpy . . . er, crazy!

"All right, all right," I said, inching back. "I'll find out for you, Kayla, but right now I have to pick out a birthday present. See you two later." I charged between them, heading for the cash register with the five-year diary and the polka-dot heart diary in my hand.

"Two diaries today?" the cashier asked.

"Yes, please," I said. "One's for my little sis, and one's for my little S.T.A.N."

She rang up the bill, looking positively puzzled.

♥   ♥   ♥

Back home, I helped Mom clean up Carrie's party mess. Actually, Uncle Jack had done most of it. Carrie wanted the streamers to stay up over the weekend. Mom didn't mind.

"Happy Birthday," I said, giving Carrie the bookstore bag.

"*Another* present?" Stephie glared at Carrie. "She's lucky."

Uncle Jack stroked Stephie's curls. "It's her birthday, Sweet Toast."

Carrie peeked inside the plastic bag. "Two diaries?"

"The fat one with the lock and key is for you," I said, pulling the polka-dot hearts one out.

"Thanks," she said, playing with the little key dangling from a red string.

"It's time you start writing down your secrets," I

said. Mom and Uncle Jack sat on the living room sofa and held hands. I could hear Nintendo tunes floating up from the family room. "Phil and Mark must be downstairs."

Uncle Jack nodded. "They're turning into Mario magicians." He chuckled that soft comfortable laugh of his.

Carrie and Stephie knelt in the middle of the living room floor checking out the diary's lock and key. Then Carrie eyed the diary in my hand. "Who's that one for?"

I flopped down on a corner of the sofa. "Oh, this is just for a little project of mine."

Carrie looked at me funny. "A secret project?"

"Sorta."

"You have too many secrets, Holly."

"Secrets are such fun," Mom said. Uncle Jack put his arm around her and she snuggled next to him. It was then I noticed the gold heart locket around Mom's neck.

"Is *this* a secret?" I leaned over to touch it.

Mom looked at Uncle Jack, and a silly little smile crept across her face. "It's our anniversary. Five weeks ago we had our first date." Uncle Jack nodded, winking at me.

Counting weeks? This was serious!

"What's for supper?" I asked, unzipping my jacket and hanging it in the closet.

"How's Guiseppe's sound?" said Uncle Jack.

"Fabulous!" I shut the closet door. "How soon?"

"Around six-thirty," Mom said.

"Perfect." There was plenty of time to work on the rewrite of my story for *Sealed With A Kiss*.

"How was the ice cream social?" Mom asked.

"It was okay."

"Just okay?" Mom asked.

I wasn't going to recap the private—and disgusting—details of the Soda Straw scene. Not now.

"Did Stan show up?" Uncle Jack asked.

"He ended up helping Andie baby-sit her brothers."

Mom's eyebrows arched. "Andie took two-year-olds to the Soda Straw?"

"Oh, she had her reasons."

"That's strange," Mom said.

It was strange only if you didn't know how Andie's mind worked. She was a master manipulator, and right now she'd do most anything to get my cousin's attention.

Uncle Jack smiled knowingly as I headed for the stairs. *He* could explain Andie's reasons to Mom.

In my room, I settled onto my window seat beside Goofey. Mom had stuck him away in my room so Uncle Jack's allergies wouldn't act up during the party.

I began my rewrite of "Love Times Two." Marty Leigh was not only the world's best mystery writer, she was also the best editor I knew. The *only* editor I knew. Still, I was impressed with her suggestions for making my story better.

At five o'clock, the doorbell rang. I heard Stan's voice as he came in. Soon, loud shrieks floated up from the family room in the lower level. Phil and Mark were probably protesting having to switch off Nintendo so Stan could watch sports. That's how seniority worked. Stan was the oldest—he had final say. Just like with Carrie and me. Thank goodness they only came over a couple times a week.

At Guiseppe's, all of us started out on our best behavior. Phil and Mark sat on either side of Stan while Uncle Jack sat next to Mom, and Stephie squeezed in on the other side of her father. Carrie and I waited as our uncle moved another table over, making room for us.

After we ordered, I studied Stephie's face. She looked just like a seven-year-old version of her mother—Aunt Marla. Having your mother die had to be the worst thing in the world. Worse than divorce. I couldn't imagine growing up without my mom. She was fabulous.

The waitress brought our soda pop around. "Special night?" she asked, smiling at Mom and Uncle Jack, who looked positively in love.

Uncle Jack pointed to Carrie. "My niece is celebrating her birthday."

"Well, happy birthday, missy. Let's see what we can do about that," the waitress said, scurrying off.

Mark blew bubbles in his soda.

"Cut it out, fish lips," Stan said, frowning.

"Leave me alone," eight-year-old Mark said.

"*That* could be arranged," Stan said, acting

sophisticated as he checked out two cute girls at another table.

Phil dumped red pepper flakes into his hand, then licked them off his palm.

"Ew!" I said. "How can you eat that stuff?"

"It's good!" said Phil, the ten-year-old with an iron tongue.

"Let me try!" Mark said, reaching for the shaker.

"Let's try our manners on for size tonight," Uncle Jack said, taking the shaker away and casting a disapproving glance at the boys. "Remember, we're out with the ladies."

Mom giggled, leaning against him. *Oh puh-leeze*, I thought. This was getting out of hand. Mom was acting like a goofy schoolgirl!

Halfway through pizza munching, the manager and all the waitresses gathered at our table. Our waitress asked Carrie her name, then the group clicked their fingers six times before singing the birthday song. Carrie soaked up the attention. Stephie looked a little jealous as she leaned on Uncle Jack's arm.

Later, after the birthday hoopla died down, Stan raised the red flag at our table. Before you could count to ten, our waitress appeared to refill his Coke glass.

Carrie gasped. "Oh, no, that reminds me!" She stared at the flag. "I forgot about my Columbus report."

"When's it due?" I asked.

"Monday. I'll never get it done in time." She

played with the little flag at our table. "This flag reminded me."

Mom looked confused. "Why the flag?"

"When Columbus got to San Salvador he put a flag in the ground to—"

"Stake his claim for Spain," I said. "You have nothing to worry about, Carrie. I remember all that stuff from grade school. I'll help you with your report."

"Goodie!" She took another slice of pizza.

A very loud *bu-u-rp* came from Phil's direction. He burst into hysterical laughter. So did Mark.

"Philip Patterson," his father said. We all stared, embarrassed. "What do you say?"

Phil turned redder than the little flag. "Excuse me, please," he mumbled.

I wanted to hide under the table. These boys needed a mother . . . and fast. Then it dawned on me: *my* mother was the only candidate so far! I shuddered. It was fine for her to have fun on dates with Uncle Jack, but all of the sudden I realized we were sitting at Guiseppe's eating pizza like a regular family! And *certain* members of the family were behaving perfectly awful.

I glared at Phil and little Mark. And at Stan, who sat between them doing absolutely nothing but stuff his face with pizza. Carrie's birthday had turned into a horrible event. Was this a sneak preview of coming attractions?

TWELVE

Later that night, I helped Carrie with her Columbus project. Thank goodness we had a set of encyclopedias. Even though they were a little outdated, they helped with dates and stuff an eighth grader forgets after five years. Even after she had her information, I continued reading.

"Thanks, Holly," Carrie said, leaving my room.

"Copy it over in your best handwriting," I said, looking up from the encyclopedia.

"Do I *have* to?"

"You want a good grade, don't you?" I closed my bedroom door and opened the bottom drawer of my dresser. The new pink polka-dotted journal was waiting to be filled with do's and don't's for Jared. I reached for it, anxious to launch the Scrutiny Test Analyzing Nascence.

An hour later the phone rang.

"It's for you, Holly," yelled Carrie.

I raced to the hall phone. "Hello?"

"Hi. It's Paula Miller."

"Hi, Paula," I said.

"Something very weird just happened," she said.

I couldn't imagine what she was talking about. "What?"

"I called Jared, you know, like you told me to."

"Uh-huh."

"He said he couldn't talk to me and please not to call back." She sighed. "It was horrible!"

I was stunned. "Maybe he was sick or something."

"He seemed okay at the ice cream social."

"You're right, he did," I said.

"What do you think's going on?" she asked breathlessly.

I didn't dare tell her. "Look, Paula, maybe he was just busy or something. Why don't you try talking to him at church tomorrow?"

"Okay. Good idea," she said. "Bye bye."

I hung up, still trying to comprehend Paula's words. Jared wouldn't take her phone call? It was unheard of. Besides, S.T.A.N. hadn't officially started yet!

♥   ♥   ♥

On Sunday, Uncle Jack picked us up for church in his sleek gray van. I slid across the soft middle seat between Carrie and Stephie. The boys sat in the back.

Mom looked radiant as we rode to our church. Uncle Jack's eyes twinkled with the usual mischief as he stopped at the first traffic light. But when I caught him watching Mom I saw more than the playful sparkle in his eyes. This was serious stuff!

Mark hollered from the back seat, right in my ear. "Tomorrow's Columbus Day!"

"No school," squealed Carrie.

"Do you have off work?" I asked Mom.

"We all do, don't we, Jack?" she said.

"Hey, we do!" he said. "Let's do something extra special together."

"Like what?" Carrie shouted.

"Like sleep in," hooted Stan from the back.

"That's boring," Phil said.

"Yeah," said Mark. "Let's go hiking instead."

"Good idea, isn't it, dear?" Uncle Jack said, turning to look at Mom.

"We could pack our lunch and take it up Copper Mountain," Mom said.

"On the gondola," Uncle Jack said.

Not that. I just barely survived the sky ride last summer. Besides, those were the days when Danny and I were good friends. I didn't want to relive those happy days. Remembering would make me feel lousy about storming out of the Soda Straw last weekend. True, Danny annoyed me with his never-ending preaching, but was that a good reason for me to freak out and totally destroy our friendship?

"I don't want to go on the gondola again," I told Mom.

"Don't be afraid," little Stephie said, holding my hand. "I'll ride with you."

Stan snickered behind me, and I whirled around. "Keep quiet," I snapped.

"What's the matter, you scared?" he taunted.

"I've been on the sky ride twice now," I said, remembering my father had said I'd gone with him when I was little.

"Well then, third time's a charm," Stan sneered.

I wanted to close his mouth permanently. Too late—our church was in sight. Uncle Jack pulled into the parking lot next to Andie's family car. Mrs. Martinez was getting one of the twins out of his car seat.

Next thing I knew, Stan had hopped out of the van and was helping her with little Chris. Talk about a splitzo schizoid! Stan was a prime example of it. If only Andie could see his nasty sneers and hear his snide remarks. But all she knew of him was *this* side of him—the Stan-to-the-Rescue side.

Andie did some fast talking and got her dad's permission to sit with Stan in church—with all nine of us in the same pew. I was watching Andie and Stan when a terrible thought hit me. What if she ever married Stanley Patterson? She'd be my cousin! The cousin part was fine; it was the wife-of-Stan part that worried me.

Soft organ music filled the church as people filed in. Across the aisle, Kayla Miller sat with her twin sister. *Someone oughta give her a crash course in being subtle*, I thought as she proceeded to gawk at Stan and Andie.

Jared and his parents came in together. He looked straight ahead as he passed the Miller twins. Poor Paula. She was going to have a tough time talking to him today!

I took a deep breath as I reached for the hymnal. Mom looked absolutely angelic sitting next to Uncle Jack on the far end of the pew. Was she ready to give up being single for this man who never believed in worrying if he didn't have to? I wondered if Daddy had any idea Mom was dating again. And not only dating again—but dating Uncle Jack—his brother-in-law!

When the sermon began, I had a hard time paying attention with zillions of thoughts racing through my mind. My cousin with my best friend? Unthinkable! My uncle with my mom? Positively scary! My first love, Jared Wilkins, with *me*? Impossible!

When church was over, the only thing I could remember was the pastor's text. It was Mark 9:50, one of the Scriptures Danny had used to get me to patch things up with my cousin, Stan—two weeks ago! Was God trying to tell me something?

The next day, Columbus Day, Uncle Jack took everyone to Copper Mountain. Everyone except Stan, who decided to stay at their house and sleep in. And me. Mom let me skip the gondola ride and go shopping with Andie instead. I'd saved up over $100 worth of baby-sitting money and wanted to get a head start on my Christmas shopping.

Andie and I hit every Columbus Day sale imaginable. Even the donut shop had a two-for-one special! By late afternoon we were exhausted. Lugging our purchases, we hopped off the bus near my house. That's when I saw a white flag stuck in our front yard.

Andie spied it too. "What's that for?" she asked.

"Beats me." I squinted to see as we came closer.

A slight breeze made it ripple as Andie ran onto the lawn, stretching the homemade banner out. "What's 'J.P.'s claim' mean?"

"Must be one of Uncle Jack's tricks," I said, wondering what he was up to now. "Let's go in and find out."

Everyone was downstairs in the family room, watching a video in the dark. "Come look," Mom said, motioning Andie and me over to the sectional. "This is Copper Mountain in the fall." The aspen were like gold against the dark evergreens.

Stephie bounced up and down. "Watch this," she said. "Here's what you missed today, Holly."

I watched as Stephie hurried into the gondola with Carrie.

"Uncle Jack took this from inside our gondola," Mom said, narrating. "Watch Stephie and Carrie wave and giggle back at us."

I watched as the cable went over the first set of terminals, making the car sway, high over the treetops. The little girls' expressions changed quickly at that point.

"That's the part I hate most," I whispered to Andie.

"That?" Andie laughed. "The swinging and swaying's the best part of the ride for me."

Soon the camera shifted to another gondola . . . behind the camera man. There sat Mark and Phil clowning around, making faces as Uncle Jack used his zoom lens to get a close-up of the younger boys.

"Is Stan here?" Andie whispered.

I shrugged. "Doesn't look like it."

When the video was finished, Uncle Jack rewound it. Then the doorbell rang and Carrie and Stephie ran to get it. Mom kept telling us over and over how beautiful the autumn was in the high country. Every time she said it, it was like she wanted to say something else. Something more important than the seasons changing. Her face glowed with excitement as she flipped on the lights.

Carrie and Stephie came racing back downstairs.

"Who was at the door?" Mom asked, leaning her head against the sectional.

"Our neighbor," said Carrie. "He wants to know what the flag in our yard is for."

"Oh, yeah," I said. "Andie and I saw it, too."

"Uncle Jack put it there," Carrie declared. "Like Columbus."

"What for?" I asked.

Uncle Jack walked across the room and grabbed a pool stick from the rack on the wall. "I'm staking my claim on Susan Meredith and her family." He stood in the middle of the family room with the pool stick in his right fist.

Stan wandered down the steps just then. "What's going on?" He stared at his father's stance. And the pool stick.

"Welcome, son," said Uncle Jack in a deeper voice than usual. "You are about to witness a historical moment."

Stan sat down in the chair across from me. What crazy antic did Uncle Jack have up his sleeve? Slouching there in his chair, Stan looked like he couldn't care less.

Uncle Jack cleared his throat. "Just as Christopher Columbus staked his claim on the newly discovered land, bringing gifts to the natives, I, Jack Patterson, do press my flag into the soil of Susan Meredith's heart."

Mom applauded the silly speech. I sat there grinning. Was this for real?

Then Uncle Jack pulled a square box from his shirt. "And now . . . a gift for the number-one native."

Mom giggled as he approached her, kneeling at her side. "She already said she'd be my wife," he told all of us. "So this makes our engagement official."

Stephie and Carrie squeezed in to see. I was sure it was a ring, but then you never know about Uncle Jack.

Mom opened the velvety lid. "Jack," she whispered, "it's beautiful!"

I slid over next to her, curious. It *was* beautiful. More than that, it was expensive! You could tell stuff like that about a diamond *this* size.

Uncle Jack took Mom's left hand in his and gently slipped the ring onto her fourth finger. He got up off his knees and playfully pulled Mom to her feet. "Ta-dah!" he said with a grand flourish, spinning her around. "Susan, we shall wed and live happily ever after."

Andie started clapping, and the rest of us joined in. "I've never been to a proposal of marriage," she said.

"Me neither," I said, laughing. "I missed Mom's first one." Oops! I hoped that didn't ruin the moment for Mom.

Carrie and Stephie joined hands with the engaged couple and Mark and Phil ran around outside the circle, trying to tickle their father. Andie and I joined in the fun, making a circle of our own. Then my uncle reached over and gave me a bear hug, the kind that used to come frequently, before Daddy left. Mom held me close.

At last, we sat down, deciding whether to celebrate by cooking cheeseburgers at home or by letting the Golden Arches do it. When I turned to look for Stan, he was gone!

THIRTEEN

The next day after volleyball practice, I rushed home to record the days' events in my S.T.A.N. diary. *Week One, Day One: It's totally shocking— Jared's ignoring every girl in school! Even Paula! I know because she came crying to me about it. Again! He's being a real jerk in a new and improved sort of way. Amazing!*

And . . . it was so weird the way he couldn't wait to meet me at the library first thing this morning. I mean, he actually seemed eager to read the requirements of S.T.A.N. and get on with the signing of it!

After supper, Kayla called with more questions about my cousin. "Holly," she pleaded. "Will you *please* find out what's going on between Andie and Stan?"

"I'll see what I can do."

"You said that before, but you didn't call back."

"I've been busy," I said, frustrated with her demands.

"Too busy to talk to your best friend . . . and call me right back?"

I sighed. "Like I said, I'll see what I can find out."

Hanging up, I wondered about Andie. Maybe I should give her a call. Nah, she'd just want to yak about Stan. On the other hand, I *should* talk to her about Jared and the secret pact she had signed promising to help me with my plan.

Andie answered on the first ring.

"Didn't see you much today," I began. "Just thought I'd call and check up on things."

"Things are cool!" she said. I was afraid she'd say that. "Stan and I are talking a lot. It's like a dream come true!"

"That's nice," I mumbled, even though it wasn't. She was too far gone over Stan to see the light now.

"I have to thank *you* for all of this," she said.

"Speaking of which," I said. "Remember our pact?"

"Sure do, and have *I* got a scheme for you."

"Like what?"

"Tomorrow I'm mailing a letter to Jared inviting him to the Harvest Festival."

"That's almost a month away, but sure, go for it."

"Whoever heard of not opening your mail," she said, laughing.

"Well, if you put your return address on it, he'll know it's from a girl. So that won't work."

"I'm one step ahead of you. No return address! How's that?"

"I get it. When he opens it, he'll *have* to read it and then we'll know he failed S.T.A.N."

"What's Stan got to do with Jared?"

Yikes! The code word slipped out! "Uh, what did I just say?" I pretended not to know.

"Something about failing Stan," she said. "Don't go getting *him* involved in this, Holly, or I'm out!"

"Don't worry, he's not involved." Suddenly I remembered Kayla's plea for information. "Uh, by the way, do you think Stan's going to ask you out?"

"Hope so. Why?"

"Just curious."

"Hey, just think, Holly. If Stan and I got married I'd not only be your best friend but your cousin. Is that cool or what?"

"Where do you come up with these things?" I asked, as if the thought had never crossed my mind.

"Never mind, I can tell you're not in the mood."

"Whatever."

"Want me to spy on Jared for you tomorrow?" she asked.

"Sure, just don't talk about it at school. Call me after volleyball, okay?"

"I'll *be* at volleyball practice tomorrow. Stan wants me to wait for him."

I still couldn't picture them together. "Okay, see you then." I hung up.

The Scrutiny Test Analyzing Nascense took most of my energy at school the next day. If I wasn't spying on Jared—checking to see if he was either failing S.T.A.N. by talking to or looking at girls—I was listening to Paula complain about the sudden change in him.

"It's not like him," she whined.

"He *does* seem different, doesn't he?" I said.

Even Billy Hill noticed. "Something's up with Jared," I overheard him say to Amy-Liz on the way to math. "He's acting strange."

By the end of the week, the whole school buzzed with rumors about Jared. One rumor had him suffering bad side effects from some medication he was taking for some rare disease I'd never heard of.

He waited at my locker Friday after school. "Hi, Holly."

It was the first I'd seen him smile all week. "This is pure torture for you, isn't it?" I asked.

"You'd be surprised," he said with a grin. "I've never had so much fun getting hit with rumors and jokes."

"Want to call the whole thing off?"

"No chance," he said, looking at me like he was sure to get me. It made me nervous—what if he *did* pass the test? Would I go out with Jared Wilkins?

Danny walked past. I turned to face my locker, avoiding him. "I've got to do something about him," I muttered into my locker, feeling a little twinge of sadness for the way things had ended between us.

"Like what?" Jared asked.

"I don't know. He looks so depressed. Maybe I should talk to him. I mean, we were such good friends before . . ."

"Has he called you?"

I shook my head. "I walked out on *him*."

"You two could talk things out and still be . . . just friends, couldn't you?"

Was Jared for real? I expected him to say something else. Something like, "Forget Danny, you've got me!" But he didn't. Instead, he handed me an envelope.

"Oh, before I forget," he said, "can you give this to Andie for me? I'm sure it's her writing."

I stared at the letter addressed to Jared. "You're right," I said, turning it over. It was unopened!

FOURTEEN

Tuesday, after lunch, I stopped off at my locker with Andie. A note stuck out of one of the little vents at the top.

"Who's it from?" Andie asked, leaning close to see.

It was from Danny—asking when we could talk. "Oh, great," I said, refolding it.

"What's wrong?"

"Danny." I opened my locker and peered at the tiny mirror stuck inside the door. "I'm a jerk, Andie," I said, fluffing my bangs with my fingers. "Danny wasn't so bad."

"You like being preached at?" She banged her locker shut. "Remember how controlling he was? Think it over, Holly. You're better off without him."

"Maybe," I said, heading for fifth period. But I wasn't absolutely sure. It was crazy, but I still liked him. Or maybe it was blind admiration. I mean, how many walking memory chips does a girl get to meet in a lifetime?

After school, Danny was waiting near the doors to the gym as I hurried in for volleyball practice. "Hi, Holly," he said softly. "Get my note?"

I nodded.

"When can we talk?"

"What about?" I asked.

His eyes were sober. "Us."

"Uh, I've got volleyball now," I said. "Miss Tucker makes us run extra laps if we're late."

"Later then?"

"I can't hang around after school today. Mom and I are going shopping for her wedding next month."

"She's getting remarried?" He seemed to brighten. "When?"

"Thanksgiving Day," I said. "And we're all dressing like pilgrims." We laughed at my dumb joke.

"Can I call you later tonight?" His eyes had sort of a pleading quality.

"Sure," I said. Just then Stan rushed past us, his whistle hanging from his neck. He shot me a strange look. "Talk to you later, Danny," I said, dashing off to the girls' locker room. Changing clothes at record speed, I made it back upstairs before Stan's whistle blew, signaling the start of practice.

Stan scowled, not only at me, but at all the girls. Good—at last even Kayla was seeing the grumpy side of him! If only Andie were here.

Halfway through practice, Jared showed up. He sat in his usual place, high in the bleachers. This S.T.A.N. thing was getting out of hand. Boys were starting to ridicule him. Certain girls were avoiding him; others were vying for his attention more than ever. Like Paula Miller, for instance.

After practice, I waited for him at the bottom of the bleachers. "Hi," I said, feeling sorry for him.

His smile warmed my heart. "Hey, Holly, you're looking good out there."

"Thanks."

"So, how am I doing?" he asked, his eyes searching mine.

"I, uh, don't know about this S.T.A.N. thing anymore," I said.

"What do you mean?" He followed me across the gym. "I agreed to it, remember? So what's the problem? I'm doing what you wanted."

I stopped to look at him. *Really* look at him. "It's all wrong, Jared. Every single part of it."

"How's it wrong?"

"Because S.T.A.N.'s turning you into a, a . . ."

Thwe-e-ep! It was Stan's whistle.

I spun around. "Now what do you want?" I yelled.

"Lay off, Holly!" Stan stood at the volleyball net, clipboard in hand, and glared at me.

I looked first at Jared, then Stan. "Huh?"

Stan folded his arms. "Keep me out of whatever it is you're talking about!"

I couldn't help but giggle. "It's nothing about *you*," I said, trying to force a straight face.

Jared grinned too. "Yeah, it's nothing, man."

I eyed my cousin, holding his precious clipboard. Driving him crazy with S.T.A.N. was perfect genius! He'd never believe we weren't talking about him—never in a zillion years!

He glared at me. "And lay off telling everyone about the wedding, too, would ya!"

"*Now* what's eating you?" I said.

"There shouldn't be a wedding at all," he said.

"You're pathetic," I shouted as he sauntered back to the bench and sat down.

"Man! What's buggin' him?" Jared said.

"He's a jerk, that's what."

"Oh," Jared said, stuffing his hands into his pockets. "Maybe you should back off from each other, Holly."

I stared at him. Now he was starting to sound like Danny—telling me what to do. "Oh, great, Jared, not *you*, too!"

Jared looked confused. "What? What did I say?"

Thoughts of S.T.A.N. whirled in my head. Jared's personality was changing—for the worse. The fun-loving Jared had disappeared. I sighed. "Maybe this scrutiny test was really one big mistake, Jared. I mean, you're *so* different. Nothing like you used to be. S.T.A.N.'s turning you into someone . . . uh, someone *awful*. And I don't like it! Maybe we should just forget the whole thing." I turned and headed for the girls' locker room.

"But Holly, wait!"

I turned around. "Not now, Jared. It's over." And this time I ran all the way down the steps to the locker room, leaving Jared standing in the middle of the gym floor.

It felt good getting away from Jared . . . and Stan. I let the water beat on my back in the shower for a long time.

♥　　♥　　♥

Thirty minutes later, Mom pulled up in front of the school. "Hi, Holly-Heart, ready to shop till we drop?"

"Can't wait," I said, settling into the front seat. "We don't have much time before your wedding, you know." I pulled a piece of paper from my purse.

Mom glanced over. "What's that?"

"We have to be organized about this if you're going to have a perfect wedding." I held my list up.

She smiled. "I should've known."

"First, we need invitations, and they must be mailed this week."

Mom looked horrified. "This week?"

"Yep. Six weeks in advance of the special day. That's *this* week." I opened my jean purse, scrounging for a pencil. "Another big item is flowers, you know. And a photographer. We must have pictures, lots of them. And . . . the food.

113

What would a Thanksgiving Day wedding be like without food? How do turkey hors d'oeuvres sound?"

"Slow down, Holly," Mom said, finding a parking space in front of Footloose and Fancy Things. "Aren't we getting ahead of ourselves? My wedding day is important, but it's not the first time, you know. Second weddings shouldn't be too showy."

"Says who? You've waited a long time for the right guy to show up. And if Daddy had been thinking straight, he'd have come to his senses and married you again instead of—"

"Holly, please. Let's not get into that."

"Do you agree with me it *has* to be special?"

She nodded. "Special, just not too fancy."

"Where's *your* list?" I waited for Mom to come around and feed the meter.

"Relax, Holly. Please? It's right here," she said, pointing to her head as we headed into my favorite shop.

Footloose and Fancy Things was the most exclusive shop in Dressel Hills. The rosy decor and soft music reminded me of a big city department store. Mirrors were everywhere. And luxurious chairs to relax in while waiting for someone to come out of the plush dressing rooms and model an outfit. That someone happened to be my mom. She deserved the best fashion critic there was— me!

Modeling a light tan dress with a gentle brocade bodice and belted waist, Mom stood before me,

114

smiling. "This is ecru," she said. "It's subtle enough to be appropriate without being white."

"Why *not* white? You can wear any color you want, Mom. And shouldn't it be longer, you know, with a train?"

Mom rolled her eyes. "Darling, maybe we should talk."

She sat down, sinking deep into the soft armchair beside me.

"I said before, second weddings shouldn't be showy." It was almost a whisper. "I haven't changed my mind."

"But you didn't have a big wedding with Daddy; why not throw a big bash with Uncle Jack?"

"Did it ever occur to you that Uncle Jack might want to have a say in the planning? This is his wedding, too."

"Okay, we'll let Uncle Jack decide a few things," I said.

Mom looked at me sideways. "Maybe you're getting too caught up in this," she muttered, hoisting herself out of the plushy chair.

As soon as she disappeared into the dressing room, I dashed to the bridal section. That's when I saw it. The perfect dress for a bride! I couldn't wait to show Mom.

When she came out to model another dress—a mint green tea-length thing with ripples for a hem—I took her arm and escorted her to the dazzling white dress with angel-wing sleeves and a train fit for a queen.

"Now *this* is you!" I stepped back, admiring the enchanting dress. "Please, Mom. Just try it on."

Mom smiled. "It's lovely, dear, but it's *not* me."

"Mo-o-m," I whined.

"I'll make you a deal," she said, lowering her voice. "I'll choose *my* wedding dress, and you choose yours. Okay?"

"That's not funny," I said. Then a fabulous idea hit me. "What about this. I'll choose the dresses for Carrie and Stephie and me to wear in the wedding. How's that?"

"Okay with me, Holly-Heart," she said, stroking my hair.

"Thanks, Mom!" Things were looking up. Mom would say almost anything now to get me off her bridal train, er, out of her hair.

While she went to try on another non-bridal look, I browsed through the juniors section of the dress shop.

The trouble with weddings is, by the time you're old enough to have one, you're too old to know what's cool and what's not. With that thought, I reached for the hot pink and purple dress calling out to me. It was all satiny pink with purple borders on the sleeves and hem, and piping around the neck. Holding it up, it was clear in an instant. I held in my hands the perfect choice for the coolest junior bridesmaids dresses in Dressel Hills. Wouldn't Mom be thrilled?

FIFTEEN

I waited with Mom as the cashier rang up her boring ecru-colored dress. "I found the perfect dress in juniors," I said. "You've got to see it, Mom. We could order three of them exactly alike, for Carrie, Stephie, and me."

Mom touched the brocade bodice of her wedding dress, apparently a zillion miles away. "That's nice," she said, handing her credit card to the clerk.

Just then Andie's mother showed up. "Shopping for your wedding, I see." She eyed Mom's purchase. "It's lovely."

Lovely? She didn't say *fabulous* or *beautiful*. The dress was definitely average—ho hum! I couldn't stand by and let Mom's wedding day be average. It had to be extra special . . . memorable. I would see to it!

Mom showed off her dress, chattering with Mrs. Martinez. Then she signed the credit card purchase slip.

"Excuse me, Mom," I said, interrupting her. "Can you come look at the dress real quick before they close?"

She was caught up with Andie's mom and wedding talk. "Here, honey, go ahead and order the dresses if you like," she said. "I'll be across the street at the florist. Meet me there." Then she handed over her credit card!

I tore off in the direction of the pink and purple dress. Just the thing to add pizzazz to a wedding that, so far, was going to be very boring.

I found the dress in the rack again. My size! On the shelves against the wall, I discovered a pair of hot pink gloves and a floral barrette. I placed the order for two more dresses—in Carrie's and Stephanie's sizes—and hurried outside. I was glad the white plastic covered the flashy dress. When we got home, I would surprise Mom and model it. She'd be so impressed with my choice. After all, weddings ought to be an occasion for celebration. Especially at Thanksgiving!

Back at home, Uncle Jack greeted us at the front door. His hair was messed up, probably from romping with the kids. Stan was at the library doing homework again. He'd been hiding out there a lot lately. Maybe he thought if he hid from reality it would go away.

"Whatcha got there, Holly?" Uncle Jack asked, trying to peek under the white plastic.

Mom intercepted. "No sneaking peeks! First look is on our wedding day."

"That goes for the *bride's* dress," he teased. "Not for the daughter of the bride's dress." He planted a kiss on my cheek.

"It's our *new* tradition, right, Mom?"

Mom looked puzzled. "Traditions are repeated customs. I don't know about Jack, but I intend for this to be *my* last wedding." Uncle Jack burst into laughter and kissed Mom. And not on the cheek, either!

With that, I dashed upstairs to model my dress. I stopped outside my door. Stuck to it was a list of phone calls. Danny's name was on it.

Uncle Jack called up from downstairs. "Holly, did you find your phone messages?"

I leaned over the banister. "Thanks, Uncle Jack."

"Looks like you need a private secretary," he teased.

Inside my bedroom, I hung up the dazzling dress and carefully removed the plastic. Then I closed the door and slipped on the most fabulous garment ever!

Standing in front of the mirror, I posed like a model. Swinging my hair up off my shoulders, I held it there, admiring the gentle gathers in the skirt and the fitted waist.

Suddenly, I remembered last Easter. Carrie had found the most incredible dress, a frilly cotton one, complete with dipped hem. But the colors weren't right for Mom. And she absolutely refused to buy the *pink and purple* Easter dress. Carrie complained and whined and nearly had a fit over it, but that didn't change Mom's mind.

I stared at the mirror, twirling myself around. I was determined to wear this dress to Mom's wedding, with exactly the same colors as the dress that got away.

"First look on the wedding day," she had said downstairs. *That goes for this dress, too*, I thought, giggling. What a sensible idea! One that would spare me from having to return three perfectly gorgeous dresses. Even if Mom didn't like the colors, everyone else would. I was sure of it.

I pulled the white plastic back over it and hung it in the back of the closet. With zillions of wedding plans on her mind, maybe Mom would forget about my purchase.

I hurried to the hall phone. Time to return phone calls—starting with Andie.

"Hi, what's up?" I said when she answered.

"Not much. Where've you been?"

"I helped Mom pick out her bride's dress today, uh, sorta. She didn't like the one that looked like a *real* bride. So we compromised. She got the one she liked, and I picked out dresses for the girls in the family."

"Matching dresses?"

"Uh-huh. The clerk said they're one of a kind, the only dresses like it in Dressel Hills!"

"That's nice, I guess." She sounded glum.

"What's wrong with you?"

"Stan. He's being a pain," she said.

I should've known. Especially after what happened today after school. "Well, you didn't believe me, Andie. He can be positively maddening sometimes."

"He's mad, all right. At his dad for getting married again." She paused. I could hear her take a breath. "And at *you*, Holly."

"At me? Again?"

"Something about you spreading stuff around about him."

I sat down in the hallway. "Well, the poor little thing can whine all he wants. The fact is, Jared and I were *not* talking about him, and that's the truth!"

"Jared? How's he fit in?"

"It's nothing, really."

"You lost me," she said. "But speaking of Jared. I ran into him after school at the Soda Straw. Amy-Liz and I popped in for a coke and there he was. Holly, he looked awful. Like someone just died."

"Really?" I felt guilty.

"Yeah, he looked miserable, so I went over to talk to him, and he wouldn't even look at me. Then I got a bright idea. I bribed Amy-Liz to go and flirt with him. And she did. But he kept his face down the whole time. Then he said the weirdest thing, without looking up."

"What?"

"He said, 'Take your flirting somewhere else. I can't talk to you now.' Can you believe it? You and your test have turned Jared into a *weirdo*."

"How do you know he said that to Amy-Liz?"

"I have proof."

I wasn't sure what she was getting at. "You what?"

"Proof. You gonna be home tonight?" she asked.

"Sure, why?"

"I'll be right over," she said, hanging up without a good-bye.

Now what? I hung up the phone. Just as I did, it rang. "Got it," I shouted to Mom. "Hello?"

"Hi, Holly." It was Daddy, calling from California! "How's everything going?"

"Fine, thanks. How are you?"

"We're fine here." It bugged me when he said *we.* "How's school?"

"Okay. Except for Stan."

"What do you mean?" he asked.

"He's causing trouble for me at school."

"Your *cousin* Stan?"

"Uh-huh."

"That's hard to picture. He's always been one of the best kids around."

"Well, he's changed."

"Does it have something to do with Uncle Jack marrying your mother?"

I held my breath. How did Daddy know? "Maybe."

"Well, I can understand it. He's worried about having two more sisters in his family." He chuckled.

"Did Grandma Meredith tell you the news about Mom?"

"Yes, and they seem very happy about your

mother getting remarried." He paused. "I've been wondering, Holly, how do you feel about Uncle Jack becoming your new father?"

I tried to swallow the rising lump in my throat. I opened my mouth, but nothing came out. *I mustn't cry*, I thought. *He'll get the wrong idea.*

"Holly, are you there?"

I coughed. "I'm okay." But my eyes were filling up with tears. "You know, Daddy, Uncle Jack will always be an uncle to me. Just because he's marrying Mom doesn't mean he'll take your place. No one could ever do that." There, now I felt better.

"I didn't intend to upset you, honey. Are you sure you're all right?"

"Uncle Jack's lots of fun. Mom's in love and everything's fine." I wondered if Daddy believed me, the way my voice sounded so quivery.

"You're crying, Holly."

"Not because I'm sad, Daddy. Really."

"Well," he said, "I'm happy for your mother. And Uncle Jack, too. He's getting a terrific wife."

I couldn't believe he said that! If that were true why didn't he stay married to Mom instead of leaving us and messing things up? I didn't say that, of course. Just asked him if he wanted to talk to Carrie. He said yes, and I ran to get her.

While Carrie talked, I sat on my window seat thinking. About Daddy's question. What made him think Uncle Jack could replace him, now or ever? I squeezed Bearie-O hard. It was then I realized he might have been upset with the news of Mom's wedding. It must be lousy finding out your wife is marrying another man. Even though she's not your wife anymore.

A knock came at my door. "Holly, you in there?" It was Andie!

I leaped off my window seat and met her. "That was fast," I said.

She pulled a Sony recorder out of her purse. "What's that for?" I asked.

"The proof I told you about. Just listen."

She pressed the play button. "Take your flirting somewhere else," said Jared's voice. "I can't talk to you now."

I stared at the recorder. "Play it back."

We listened again. "Jared doesn't sound like himself anymore," Andie said.

I nodded, stunned. "When did all this happen?"

"An hour after volleyball practice. Stan and I studied at the library, then he took the bus home and I met Amy-Liz at the Soda Straw. That's when we saw Jared."

"Does Jared know Amy-Liz was taping him?" I asked, curling up on my bed.

"See this tiny mike? It was hidden in her purse along with the tape recorder. Clever, don't you think?"

"Wow."

She put the tape recorder in its case and slipped it back into her purse. Then she sat on the floor, leaning her head on my bed. "Looks like *I'm* keeping my end of our secret pact."

"There's no need for it now." I looked up at the canopy overhead.

Andie leaned on her elbows, staring at me with her brown saucer eyes. "Why not?"

I was close to telling her that Jared's test was called off when the phone rang. "I'll be right back." I raced to the hall.

"Hello?" I said.

"Hi, Holly. It's Jared."

"Hi," I said, wondering why *he* was calling.

"I've been thinking."

"Yeah?"

"I'm confused about something."

I sneaked down the hall to see if Andie was overhearing my end of the conversation. "Like what?"

"Like the reason you're so mad at me for following all the rules on your list. It has to mean only one thing."

"What thing?" I waited.

He took a deep breath. "Like maybe you never wanted me to pass S.T.A.N. in the first place."

"You think that?" I said, feeling a little jittery inside. "How come?"

"It's this feeling I have, Holly. Like you agreed to S.T.A.N. just for the fun of it. Am I right?"

"Of course not, Jared. But I really think we should just forget about S.T.A.N. It was a dumb idea. Look, I have a friend over. I'll talk to you later, okay? Bye." I whirled around to hang up the phone, only to meet Andie's scowl.

"What do you mean 'forget about Stan,' Holly?"

she shouted. "This must be what Stan was talking about today!" She grabbed my arm and pulled me into my bedroom. She pointed to my window seat. "Sit down, girl. It's time we talked."

"There's nothing to talk about, Andie. Honest!"

Her hands were on her hips. "I *heard* what you said."

"What you *thought* you heard was nothing about Stan."

"I heard you say his name to Jared." Her eyes were boring a hole into me.

"You were hearing things." I crossed my legs under me.

"You're calling me a liar, aren't you?"

"You're all mixed up, Andie. Forget it."

"I'm going to get to the bottom of this, Holly. And you can't stop me." She reached for her purse.

"Where are you going?" I said, bounding off the window seat and following her to my bedroom door.

"To Jared's. He's going to talk to me whether he likes it or not!" And she slammed the bedroom door in my face.

I felt like I'd been punched in the stomach. By my very best friend!

SIXTEEN

At school the next day, another note was stuck on my locker. *Danny doesn't quit*, I thought as I read it. My mother's wedding was more than a month away and he was asking me to let him escort me "as a friend."

Then in comp class, Jared passed me a note. It said the exact same thing! I wondered what would happen if I said I'd go with *both* guys? I almost wished I could!

Funny, for a girl who was hardly noticed by boys last year, I had come a long way! I grinned to myself. If Danny knew what I was thinking, he'd be quoting Proverbs and the verse about pride going before destruction.

At lunch, I sat at a table alone. Danny was nowhere to be seen. But Jared was. He came right over and sat beside me. He started in without saying hi. "It's okay with me, Holly, if you want to officially call off the scrutiny test. But at least give me credit for one thing."

"What?" I bit into my chicken salad sandwich.

"At least say I passed S.T.A.N."

He had a point. "You *are* amazing, Jared. How'd you change yourself like this?"

"I wanted to convince you to be my girlfriend by following your plan. And you're right, Holly—it *was* stupid. But stupid or not, I agreed to it and so did you. So I've decided to keep my part of the deal until Thanksgiving."

He wasn't kidding! I could tell by the serious look in his eyes.

"Well, if *you* want to, okay. But count me out."

"Wait a minute, Holly. You agreed to this thing, too." He looked a little peeved.

I picked at the chips on my plate, not saying anything.

Jared snapped his fingers. "I've got it! Maybe *you* could become a scrutiny test victim. I'll create a test to analyze perfection . . . in Holly Meredith. What do you say?"

I felt ridiculous, actually. Jared was right, I wasn't perfect—I just acted like I thought I was. "Go ahead," I said. "Make your list. What do I have to do?"

He opened his spiral notebook. "Number one," he said as he wrote it, "Love the Lord with all your heart." He flashed his wonderful smile at me.

I giggled.

He started to write again. "Number two. Love your neighbor as yourself."

I could see what he was getting at. I'd treated some of my "neighbors" pretty lousy. Including my cousin Stan.

He clicked his pen and ripped the paper out, handing it to me. "That's all, Holly. That's my list."

"Are you sure you and Danny haven't traded personalities?" I reached for my Coke. "You're starting to sound awful preachy."

He grinned. "Danny and I have more than one thing in common now." And then he did it—he winked that gloriously flirtatious wink of his!

I leaned forward. "You're back, Jared! You're really in there, aren't you?"

He tilted back in his chair. "What can I say, Holly-Heart?"

I liked him better already. Maybe I *would* let him escort me to the wedding after all.

Stan came through the line and headed for our table. "Hey, Holly," he called. He sat down without an invitation. "I don't know what's going on between you and Andie, but she's freaked out. Can you straighten this mess out with her?" It wasn't a question—it was a command.

Jared looked at me, then tapped the paper I held in my hand, reminding me of his list. *Love your neighbor as yourself*—it rang in my ears.

I sighed, then smiled. "I'll see what I can do."

Stan looked shocked. "You will?"

"Uh-huh." I smiled at him . . . for a change.

His eyes softened for a second. "Thanks, cuz."

It wasn't easy taking orders from an older cousin, especially one with an attitude problem. But Jared let me know I did the right thing by winking at me again. I felt absolutely fabulous.

Paula and Kayla wandered over. "This looks like the place to be," Kayla cooed, eyeing Stan.

Paula eyed Jared. "No one's having half as much fun as you three," she said.

"Have a seat," I said as Jared slid over next to me making room for Paula. Lots of room.

Kayla sat across from us, beside Stan.

Jared turned his attention back to me. "When's that story of yours coming out, Holly?" he asked.

"Next month," I said, pushing my hair back.

"I'm going to read it, you know," he said.

"Okay," I said, gathering up my trash. I could see by the desperate look in Paula's eyes that she was dying for a chance to talk to Jared alone. So I excused myself and left.

When I got to my locker, there was Andie, pacing. She grabbed my arm as usual. "Talk to me, Holly, 'cause Jared won't."

"You really went over there last night?"

"For about five seconds." She opened her locker.

"That's weird."

"Jared refused to see me. His mother said so."

"Sounds like he's sticking to his end of the deal."

"So are you gonna tell me why you're spreading

130

stuff around about your own cousin? It's making me mad."

"I can only tell you one thing, Andie," I said. "I was *not* talking about my cousin to Jared yesterday. It's the honest truth and if you can't trust your best friend, then go ahead and think what you want."

She stared at me, her dark eyes beginning to squint like Mom's when she's upset. "You better not be lying!"

"I'm not, honest."

"Then why did I hear you talking about Stan on the phone with Jared yesterday?"

I could see she wouldn't let it go. "Promise you'll keep a secret?"

"I promise." Andie waited, breathless for my response.

"Stan is a code word, an abbreviation for Scrutiny Test to Analyze Nascence."

"Huh?" Andie looked bewildered.

"It's a long story, Andie."

"Why'd you need a code word?" she asked.

"So no one would know what Jared and I were discussing."

"I get it! People would think you were talking about your cousin."

I nodded.

"Makes sense," she said.

"Remember, Andie, not one word to Stan about this."

Just then Jared and Stan walked past, grinning at us as they headed to their lockers. Minus the

Miller twins! I watched as Jared moved down the hall, away from us.

Andie poked me. "Daydreamer, wake up. Drooling over your first love?"

I shrugged my shoulders.

"I bet you end up with him when your silly scrutiny test is over."

"Can't decide," I said, touching up my hair. "Besides, there's something even more important than Jared right now."

Andie was all ears. "Who? Someone new?"

"It's my cousin, silly. I want to make sure things improve between us before the wedding. We're gonna be living in the same house together soon."

"So have you planned the perfect wedding for your mother?" She pulled out her books for the next period.

"It's not easy planning weddings. Mom wants to keep things simple."

"Who's in it?" she asked, stacking up her books.

"Mom's friend from work is the matron of honor. Stan's the best man. And all six of us kids will stand up with them. That was Uncle Jack's idea.

"Who's giving her away?"

"Nobody."

"That's weird."

"She's old enough to give herself away, don't you think?"

"I guess," she said. "Can I come?"

"Of course, silly. *Everyone's* invited."

"Really? Who?"

"Well . . . the Miller twins since they knew Uncle Jack back east, and Danny and Jared and—"

Andie looked shocked. "*Both* of them?"

"Yeah," I said laughing. "And they both want to escort me!"

Andie smirked. "Well, let's hear it for Miss Popularity."

I mumbled, "Yeah, yeah."

Danny showed up just then and asked to walk me to fifth hour. "Sure," I said as he reached for my books. It almost felt like the old days, before—

"I called you yesterday, but you were gone. Did you get the message?" he asked.

"Yeah, and I started to call you back, but something came up."

"Can we talk now?"

I nodded. "I got your note."

"Well, what do you think?"

"It's not a good idea," I said.

"Why not?" He stopped dead in his tracks in the middle of the busy hallway.

"Because weddings are, you know, places to hang out with . . . uh . . . *everyone.*"

"I get it," he said, opening the classroom door for me. "You have other plans, like maybe with Jared, right?"

He was partly right. But I didn't want to hurt his feelings more than I already had. "I do accept your offer of friendship, Danny. Let's be good friends again like we were before."

A broad grin stretched across his face. "Sure, Holly. That'd be great!"

As Danny turned to leave, Jared walked past. In front of him stood Paula, Amy-Liz, and Shauna, all trying to force him to look at them. He grinned at *me*, refusing to glance at the girls blocking his way!

Giggling, I turned and hurried to find a seat in math.

Jared was perfectly amazing. If he really wanted to continue S.T.A.N. till Thanksgiving, it was okay with me.

Right now it was hard to focus on what the teacher was saying. I could still see Jared flirting with me at lunch, and I was secretly relieved. The *real* Jared was back!

SEVENTEEN

That night, Uncle Jack came over with all four kids. He made popcorn—enough for a houseful of snack-crazy children and two lovey dovey adults. Everyone sat around the family room while Mom and Uncle Jack chose their wedding music from a tape of The Brooklyn Tabernacle Choir. For a minute, I thought the walls were going to cave in, especially when Uncle Jack turned up the volume on "To God Be the Glory."

Who could sit still with the sounds of the upbeat choir vibrating through the house? Phil sat in a blue beanbag, moving his head to the beat. "Sounds like this might be a cool wedding, after all," he said.

"You can say that again," Uncle Jack said, giving Mom a squeeze.

I thought of the pizzazzy dresses I'd ordered yesterday. If Mom and Uncle Jack could walk down the aisle after the ceremony to soul music, I could wear celebration colors like hot pink and purple.

Stan clicked his fingers to the beat while his brothers threw popcorn at each other's mouths. It felt good having Stan around for a change. He was being nice to practically everyone. Everyone except our cat, Goofey.

"This cat's got to go," he said, picking him up. "Dad's allergic to him. And . . . he's ugly." He was serious!

I crawled over the floor and rescued Goofey from Stan, cuddling him like a baby. "That's why we named him Goofey. He's not a regular-looking cat. He's goofy looking."

Stan laughed. "No kidding."

Uncle Jack sneezed three times then dug into his pants pocket, finding his allergy pill and popping it into his mouth. He swallowed it without water.

Carrie stared at him, wide-eyed. "How do you *do* that?"

Mark laughed out loud. "Ever hear of spit?"

"Gross," Carrie said.

"Yeah, gross," Stephie said.

"That's nothin'," Phil began. "Watch this." He started to pull his eyelid up.

"Never mind, son," Uncle Jack said, sparing us from Phil's eyeball removal trick.

After they went home, Mom knocked on my

bedroom door. "Holly, can you model your dress for me now?"

I opened the door. "Uh, how about tomorrow?" I said, hoping she wouldn't push the issue. Maybe she'd forget by then. Tomorrow she had appointments with the caterer and the organist.

"That's fine, Holly-Heart. Sweet dreams." She kissed my forehead.

"You too, Mom." She headed down the hall to tuck Carrie in. Phew—close call! Grabbing my nightshirt and robe, I headed for the shower to do some fast thinking about stalling tactics . . . just in case!

The caterer appointment took longer than Mom planned on Thursday, so she put off meeting with the organist till Friday. By then, she'd completely forgotten about seeing my dress. It was a good thing, too. Carrie's and Stephie's dresses were ready to be picked up at Footloose and Fancy Things—special ordered from Denver! Now if I could just keep them hidden till the day of the wedding, things would be perfect.

A whirlwind of days spun past as Thanksgiving Day approached. I decided to tell Jared *no thanks* to his invitation to escort me to Mom's wedding. And Mom? She was a giddy but happy bride-to-be. Uncle Jack was his comfortable, take-things-in-stride self.

Grandpa and Grandma Meredith arrived two days before the wedding. They didn't seem to mind camping out in the family room, where the sectional pulled out to a queen-sized bed. Gifts were piled up everywhere. Mom was getting married to Uncle Jack and everything seemed to be going along at a near-perfect pace.

Stephie and the boys moved their stuff in the day before the wedding. Ever since they moved to Dressel Hills, they'd been living in an apartment until Uncle Jack could find a house to buy. And now they were coming to live with us!

The trouble with weddings is when your mom marries a man with four kids, reality whacks you on the head sooner or later. For me, the reality whack came as losing my privacy! Mom showed up for a heart-to-heart chat about it.

"Carrie and Stephie will have to share your room, dear," she began, almost apologetically.

I felt betrayed. "Oh, Mom, no!"

"The boys will bunk in Carrie's old room, for a while."

"What do you mean, for a while?"

She sat on the bed beside me. "I know you won't like this, Holly, but we need to move to a bigger house soon."

"What's wrong with *this* house?" I sank back against a mountain of pillows and stared at the underside of the canopy. Feelings of panic swept over me.

"We haven't decided anything yet, dear." Mom leaned back on the bed, close to me. "Please, don't worry about it, Holly-Heart. Now's a happy time. Okay?"

Carrie and Stephie came in the room without knocking, dumping a pile of clothes and stuffed animals on my window seat. "There, that's a good place for now," Carrie said.

Then Stephie turned to me, holding something behind her back. "I, uh, snooped in your drawer, Holly," she said. "And I found this." She held out the polka-dot hearts journal with the weekly record of S.T.A.N. in it.

"You little sneak!" I yelled.

"I-I'm sorry, Holly. When I found it, I thought it belonged to my brother. But then I gave it to him and—"

I flew off the bed. "You showed this to *Stan*?"

She stepped back, away from me. "He said it wasn't his, that I should give it back to you."

"Mom?" I pleaded. "Do something, please!"

Mom stood up slowly. "Girls, I'd like both of you to meet me in the kitchen."

"Okay, Aunt Susan," Stephie said. She left the room with Carrie, both of them giggling as they ran down the steps.

"There's no way your sleeping arrangement will work, Mom! I won't tolerate Stephie's constant snooping." I felt tears filling my eyes, but I angrily brushed them away.

"Let's not worry about sleeping arrangements just now," Mom said. "The wedding comes first. We'll work out the plans for the new house soon enough." She left the room, a spring in her step.

Let's not worry. That was easy for *her* to say. My father had built this house. It was the only house

139

I'd ever known. Everything I loved was here. I scuffed my feet against the rug as I headed for my window seat. Nearly sacred, this spot had served as my private corner of the world. Secret lists were written here. And stories and journal entries. Letters to pen pals and notes to boyfriends . . . and zillions of prayers. Tons of them had already been answered.

I sat down in my favorite place, fighting the urge to shove Stephanie's pile of clothes off, onto the floor. But in the corner, crumpled up, was the dress she had worn to her mother's funeral, over nine months before. I could almost see Stephie's swollen eyes, her tear-stained face. Guilt swept over me. *Now's a poor time to be angry at her*, I thought as I folded up her clothes carefully.

Thanksgiving Day came early at the soon-to-be Meredith and Patterson household. Mom drove to the church to meet with her matron-of-honor. The florist and caterer would be waiting for last-minute instructions.

I was responsible for getting Carrie ready. Stephie, too. Uncle Jack dropped her off early. The girls couldn't wait to put on their fancy dresses.

"It's that Easter dress from last year!" Carrie said. "The one Mommy didn't like."

"No, it's not. Now stand still," I said, buttoning her up. "We have to be ready soon. Uncle Jack's picking us up in forty minutes."

Stephie ran down the steps in her flouncy dress. "Here, kitty kitty," she called.

"Goofey's down here," Grandpa called from the kitchen.

"Why's she want Goofey?" I asked Carrie.

"Because Uncle Jack said he could be in the wedding." She ran downstairs after her cousin.

Goofey in the wedding? Who ever heard of such a dumb thing! Besides, Uncle Jack was allergic to him. I fluffed my bangs and sprayed them again. Then I snapped the floral barrette into my hair, put on my hot pink gloves, and posed for the mirror. "Absolutely smashing," I said.

Grandma's eyebrows arched when she saw the dresses. "Your mother's taste in clothing seems to have changed recently."

"Aren't they beautiful?" Carrie said, spinning around, making the skirt puff out a little.

Stephie carried Goofey into the living room. She held him while Carrie put the leash on him.

"You're not *really* taking this cat to Mom's wedding, are you?" I said.

"Don't worry so much, Holly. It'll be okay," Carrie said.

"Yeah." Stephie nodded. "Daddy says the whole family has to be in the wedding. Right, Carrie?"

"Just ask Uncle Jack if you don't believe us," Carrie said, showing off in front of Grandpa and Grandma.

With Goofey on a leash, we climbed into Uncle Jack's van and sped off. There was still a good chance Mom's wedding could be absolutely perfect. I would hide Goofey in one of the Sunday school storage cupboards!

At the church, Mom was hidden away somewhere getting dressed in that boring ecru-colored thing. Carrie, Stephie and I waited in the usher's room just off the foyer. Grandma waited with us. How could I get Goofey out of the room? I *had* to make sure the wedding went off without this cat spoiling everything.

I picked him up, heading for the door. "Goofey's got some dirt on his whiskers."

"You'd better stay here," Grandma said. "Time's getting short. Goofey looks fine to me."

My heart sank as I stood there holding him. I stared at the gold and orange lace around his neck. "Where'd he get this fancy collar?"

Stephie came over to pet him. "It matches the wedding flowers," she said. "That's where."

Gold and apricot? Aargh! I stared at the three of us in our hot pink and purple. Mom would have a fit—no question!

"Three minutes and counting," Stan said, poking his head into the room, handing over our gold and apricot nosegays. "Man, do *they* clash." He frowned and shook his head as he closed the door.

I swallowed hard. This was supposed to be Mom's special day. A day to remember. *She'll remember, all right.* I looked at my watch—time to line up.

In the hallway, I noticed Billy Hill, dressed up as never before. I'd invited everyone from the youth group, but I was surprised to see him here, especially since he'd been avoiding Andie and me ever since their breakup. He smiled as I walked past him toward the foyer of the church.

Mom stood in the foyer, just outside the double doors leading to the sanctuary. She held a bouquet of apricot-colored flowers. When she saw our dresses she let out a tiny high-pitched squeak. Her hand quickly covered her mouth as her eyes stared in horror. Then the matron-of-honor stifled a giggle. So did Carrie. Soon, Mom was holding her sides, laughing. It was a good thing the organ swelled to a loud crescendo right then.

That was our cue. The matron-of-honor began to move down the aisle, between the pews decorated with *golden* mums and *apricot*-colored carnations. I was next. I wanted to toss away my clashing flowers, but I needed something to hold onto as I walked the aisle.

A gentle wave of snickers filled the church as the guests viewed the crazy color combination. I cringed. So much for the perfect wedding.

Halfway down the aisle, I cringed even more. There sat Kayla Miller, wearing a dress exactly like mine! Exclusive, one-of-a-kind deal? Right! I held my breath to keep from freaking out.

On the bride's side of the church sat Danny with his parents. He looked handsome in his brown dress slacks and tan sweater vest. When he smiled, I knew we were still friends in spite of everything. Two rows ahead of Danny, sat Jared with Paula Miller! He looked drop-dead gorgeous in a new dark suit. But *she* was wearing *another* dress just like mine. My legs felt rubbery as I made my way to the front of the church.

This was outrageous. I wanted to hide under the altar. Instead, I took my place beside the matron-of-honor, turning to face the crowd.

Out there, in a sea of faces, Paula was grinning at Jared. He smiled back at her. It was the last day of the scrutiny test—and he'd completely blown it!

EIGHTEEN

In a total state of panic, I watched as Carrie came down the aisle. Next was Stephie, with Goofey on a leash. A not-so-soft stream of laughter rippled through the crowd as they crept to the altar.

At last, all eyes were on my mother. She wore the sweetest smile in the world. Uncle Jack's gaze met hers as he followed her with his eyes. Stan, the best man, and Phil and Mark stood at rapt attention.

"Dearly beloved," the minister began as Mom took Uncle Jack's arm at the altar.

A quick glance at Goofey made me shudder. He was curled up on the groom's shiny black shoes! Uncle Jack pinched his nose closed with his right hand, stifling a sneeze. He searched first one pocket then another for a handkerchief.

Oh great, I thought, *he's forgotten to take his allergy pills!* Mom looked concerned, but Uncle Jack blew his nose and smiled. The ceremony continued.

Mark stood quieter than I'd ever seen him. Then I noticed he'd locked his knees. Mom had warned all of us at rehearsal, "Keep your knees bent during the ceremony. You'll be able to stand still longer without getting tired."

It was obvious Mark had forgotten.

While the vocalist sang The Lord's Prayer, Mom and Uncle Jack bowed their heads, holding hands. Seeing them together like this gave me a warm feeling inside, even in spite of the hot pink and purple dresses with apricot and golden bouquets. In spite of the cat. And in spite of Jared sitting with Paula!

Just as the singer was finishing her last, long "amen," Mark silently slumped to the platform. He'd blacked out! Mom gasped. In a second, Stan scooped him up and carried him out. Uncle Jack remained calm and reassured Mom with a wink.

What else could go wrong? I swallowed hard, wishing this wedding were over.

The most solemn moment of the ceremony was about to begin—the repeating of the vows. Uncle Jack blew his nose again. I wanted to cry.

When the minister asked, "Do you Jack Patterson take Susan Meredith to be your lawfully wedded wife?" Uncle Jack opened his mouth to say "I do" but "Ah-ah, I, uh, *ah-choo!*" came out instead. The guests applauded.

The perfect wedding was turning into a three-ring circus!

Three rings are better than none, I thought as the latest problem presented itself. Stan was outside with Mark—and he had the ring!

"What token of love do you wish to present to your bride?" the minister asked.

Uncle Jack reached into his coat pocket. Then both pants pockets. I saw the twinkle in his eye. Was he trying to fool the audience? He shrugged his shoulders . . . no ring! Then, ever-so-slowly he reached up behind Mom's ear and with a grand flourish produced an elf ring! With hot pink hair!

The guests burst into applause again. Things quieted down soon enough while Uncle Jack placed the cereal box ring on Mom's finger, slightly above her elegant diamond.

They kissed longer than ever. Finally, the minister presented them as Mr. and Mrs. Jack and Susan Patterson. The soulful strains began as the bride and groom started the recessional.

Goofey refused to be led on his leash, so I handed my bouquet to Phil and carried the cat down the longest church aisle in the world. The minute my feet touched the foyer, I raced to the rest room. Goofey hid under a chair in the waiting area of the posh ladies' room.

Andie showed up in a flash. "That was the best wedding ever!" she announced.

I stared at her in disbelief. "How can you say that?"

"Because it was."

147

Kayla Miller came in, minus her usual grin, and glared at my dress. "My sister and I were told these were the only dresses like this in Denver."

"Denver? You went *there* to get them?" I said. She nodded.

"No wonder," I muttered, fluffing my bangs.

"Hey, don't let it bug you," Andie said. "You're so lucky, Holly. Your Uncle Jack is one of the coolest guys around."

Kayla agreed. "Did you see how he pulled that crazy ring out of her mom's ear?"

That's all they could talk about—the wacky wedding. I slipped out of the rest room when they weren't looking. The stress was making me hungry. Besides, I had to know what Jared was doing with Paula Miller on the final day of scrutiny.

I headed for the reception hall hoping to sneak a snack. Mr. Ross, my science teacher, was working in the kitchen. Then Miss Wannamaker, my creative writing teacher, came around the corner, carrying punch glasses. Was I dreaming?

"Oh, hello there, Miss Holly," Mr. Ross said, spying me. "What can I do for you, young lady?"

"Oh nothing," I said, sitting down, feeling dizzy.

"Look. She's exhausted," Miss W said, bringing a tray of hors d'oeuvres around.

"Did you have a good breakfast today?" Mr. Ross asked.

I remembered vaguely some juice and toast early this morning. I nodded. Didn't want him to think I was neglected.

As I looked up, I noticed his hot pink tie. Something was up! Mr. Ross owned only one tie— the one he wore every single day of his life. Then I noticed his smudgy glasses were missing. He was wearing contacts! I looked from Mr. Ross to Miss W. They were smiling at each other, oblivious to me. So *that* was it. Mr. Ross was in love! I took a bite of cracker.

Then I heard someone behind me say my name. It was Jared.

"Hi," he said, sitting beside me. "Some wedding."

"Yeah," I whispered.

"I hope ours is half as much fun." He winked at me.

I blushed. "You can't be serious."

"We have more in common than I thought." He pulled the first issue of *Sealed With A Kiss* out of his pocket. "You are *some* writer, Holly!"

"Where'd you get this?" I asked, puzzled about the magazine.

He found my story without saying a word. There it was—"Love Times Two"!

"Wow, look at that. I'm really published!" My name was under the title in big letters. I read halfway through before stopping.

"How's it feel?" he asked.

"Fabulous!"

"Are you ready for this?" He turned the page.

I studied the two-page spread. It was a story called "Love Minus One." The author's name was Janeen Williams. "Who's that?"

"My new *pen name*," he said, grinning.

"Jared Wilkins, you're crazy!"

"About you," he said, touching my hand. "Let's collaborate."

"On a story?" I looked into his mischievous face. Something else was on his mind!

"You figure it out," he said, as the wedding party made its appearance.

"Not till you explain some things first. How come Paula was sitting next to you?"

"Oh, that." He flipped the hair back from his eyes. "It was Paula's idea. She came in and sat right down. When I started to get up and leave, my dad gave me the evil eye . . . and you know the rest."

I believed him, I absolutely did! "Well as far as I'm concerned, Jared, you've passed S.T.A.N. with flying colors. Whenever you want to start acting like yourself *all* the time—"

"If you don't mind, I think I'll carry on as is." He straightened his tie.

I gasped. "What did you just say, Jared?"

He stared blankly, trying to act innocent.

"Jared Wilkins—what you said—it was a direct quote from my story on metamorphosis for Miss Wannamaker's class!"

He looked sheepish. "Uh, yeah, I guess it was."

"What's going on?" I demanded.

"I'm sorry about that, Holly." He told me about the day he snooped in my locker. "It's just that when I saw your locker open . . . and your essay, I got the idea to change myself . . . exactly the way you wrote it in your assignment."

"So that's why the pages were out of order. Why you!" Andie was right about one thing. I *had* created a monster. "Jared," I said. "S.T.A.N.'s over now. You can cut the serious routine any time. Please?"

"Okay, Holly-Heart, how's this?" he said, offering his arm.

"Much better," I whispered, slipping my pink gloved hand through the bend in his elbow as he escorted me to the receiving line. Then he stepped back into the crowd, blowing a kiss. The scrutiny test monster was gone—forever, I hoped!

I took my place in the family lineup for the photographer. Uncle Jack held the bride's hand as the camera clicked. I'd never seen such love sparkles in Mom's eyes. Perfect or not, this was a day to remember.

I smiled for the camera. But deep inside I worried, just a little. About having to share my room with two tiny snoopers, and about trying to survive with three *boys* living in my house.

That's the trouble with weddings—you don't exactly know how things are going to work out. But you hope—with all your heart—that it's very close to *and they all lived happily ever after!*

♥ About the Author ♥

Beverly Lewis remembers walking the wedding aisle as a three-year-old flower girl. She forgot to drop the rose petals until she saw her mother.

At ten, Beverly played the piano for a house wedding. (Her father was a minister.) When the bride and groom showed up without a musician, Beverly performed her recital pieces instead of wedding music. The couple never even noticed! Since then, Beverly has played everything from classical to ragtime at big church weddings.

Goldie and Angie—Beverly's childhood cats— weren't allowed inside for the house wedding, so she doesn't know if the groom would have had a sneezing fit or not.

A former schoolteacher, Beverly has published articles and short stories in such magazines as *Highlights For Children, Brio, Faith 'N Stuff, Teen Power,* and *Dolphin Log.* Her hilarious chapter books are titled *Mountain Bikes and Garbanzo Beans* and *The Six-Hour Mystery.* And she is the author of the *Cul-de-sac Kids* series of chapter books.